TATER TALES

the KING of the World!

Ben Clanton

SIMON & SCHUSTER BOOKS FOR YOUNG READERS
NEW YORK   LONDON   TORONTO   SYDNEY   NEW DELHI

FOR HIS MAJESTY KING THEO! YOU'RE ROYALLY AWESOME!

SIMON & SCHUSTER BOOKS FOR YOUNG READERS
An imprint of Simon & Schuster Children's Publishing Division
1230 Avenue of the Americas, New York, New York 10020
This book is a work of fiction. Any references to historical events, real people, or real places are used fictitiously. Other names, characters, places, and events are products of the author's imagination, and any resemblance to actual events or places or persons, living or dead, is entirely coincidental.
© 2024 by Ben Clanton
Stock photos and illustrations by iStock
Book design by Lucy Ruth Cummins
All rights reserved, including the right of reproduction
in whole or in part in any form.
SIMON & SCHUSTER BOOKS FOR YOUNG READERS and related marks
are trademarks of Simon & Schuster, LLC.
For information about special discounts for bulk purchases,
please contact Simon & Schuster Special Sales at 1-866-506-1949
or business@simonandschuster.com.
The Simon & Schuster Speakers Bureau can bring authors to your live event.
For more information or to book an event, contact the Simon & Schuster Speakers Bureau at
1-866-248-3049 or visit our website at www.simonspeakers.com.
The text for this book was set in Typewriter.
The illustrations for this book were rendered in Procreate,
watercolors, potato stamps, photographs, and Photoshop.
Manufactured in China
1124 SCP
First Simon & Schuster Books for Young Readers paperback edition April 2025
2 4 6 8 10 9 7 5 3 1
Library of Congress Cataloging-in-Publication Data
Names: Clanton, Ben, 1988- author, illustrator.
Title: King of the world! / Ben Clanton.
Description: New York : Simon & Schuster Books for Young Readers, 2024. | Series:
Tater tales ; 2
Identifiers: LCCN 2023027938 (print) | LCCN 2023027939 (ebook) | ISBN 9781534493216
(hardcover) | ISBN 9781534493223 (paperback) | ISBN 9781534493230 (ebook)
Subjects: CYAC: Graphic novels. | Humorous stories. | Potatoes-Fiction.
Friendship-Fiction. | BISAC: JUVENILE FICTION / Comics & Graphic Novels / Humorous |
JUVENILE FICTION / Social Themes / Friendship | LCGFT: Humorous comics. | Graphic novels.
Classification: LCC PZ7.7.C556 Ki 2024 (print) | LCC PZ7.7.C556 (ebook)
DDC 741.5/973-dc23/eng/20231211
LC record available at https://lccn.loc.gov/2023027938
LC ebook record available at https://lccn.loc.gov/2023027939

CHAPTER 1: **IN SEARCH OF A SPUDDY** VIII

CHAPTER 2: **HOLEY MOLEY** 12

CHAPTER 3: **KING ME!** 26

CHAPTER 4: **DOWN WITH THE KING** 40

CHAPTER 5: **THE AMENDS** 54

SPUDTACULAR FACTS AND FUN 69

CHAPTER 1
IN SEARCH OF A SPUDDY

This is Rot Poe Tater. He is one excited mutant potato. Why is Rot so excited?

Because today Rot has decided to go . . .

SPUDLUNKING!

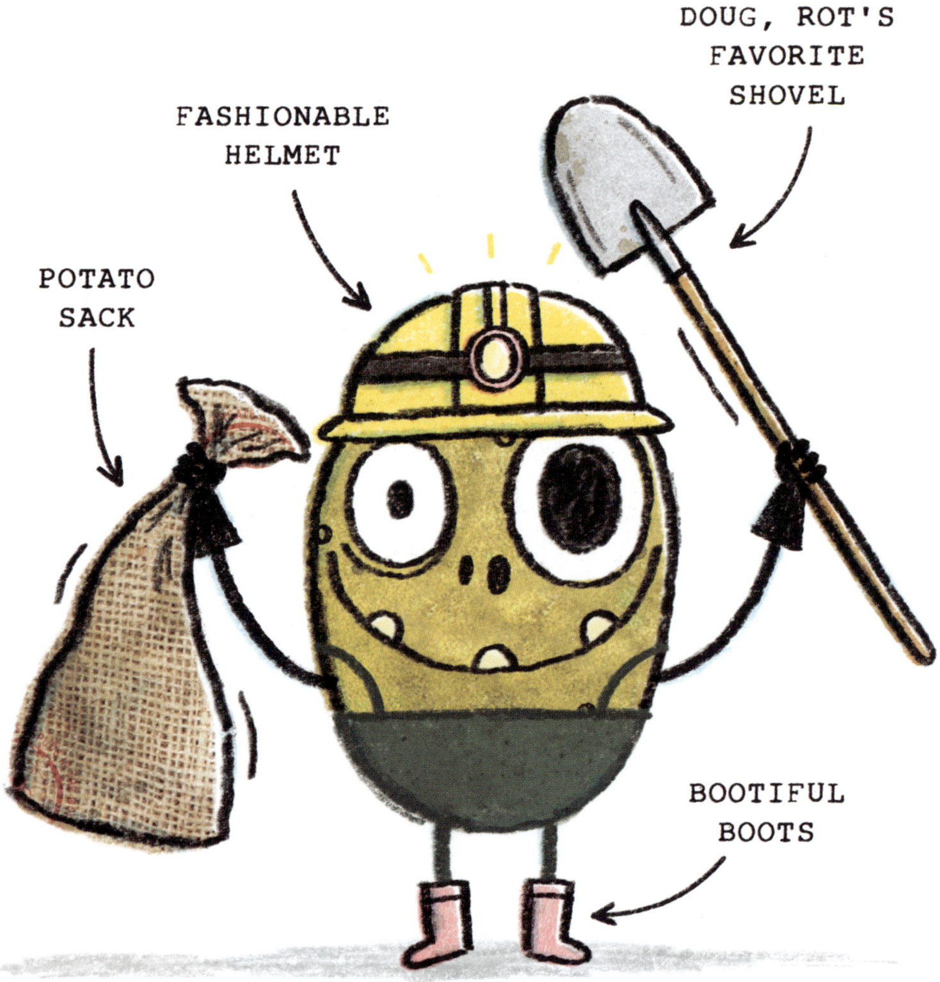
DOUG, ROT'S
FAVORITE
SHOVEL
FASHIONABLE
HELMET
POTATO
SACK
BOOTIFUL
BOOTS

What is spudlunking? Perhaps you are familiar with spelunking? A recreational pastime of exploring cave systems?

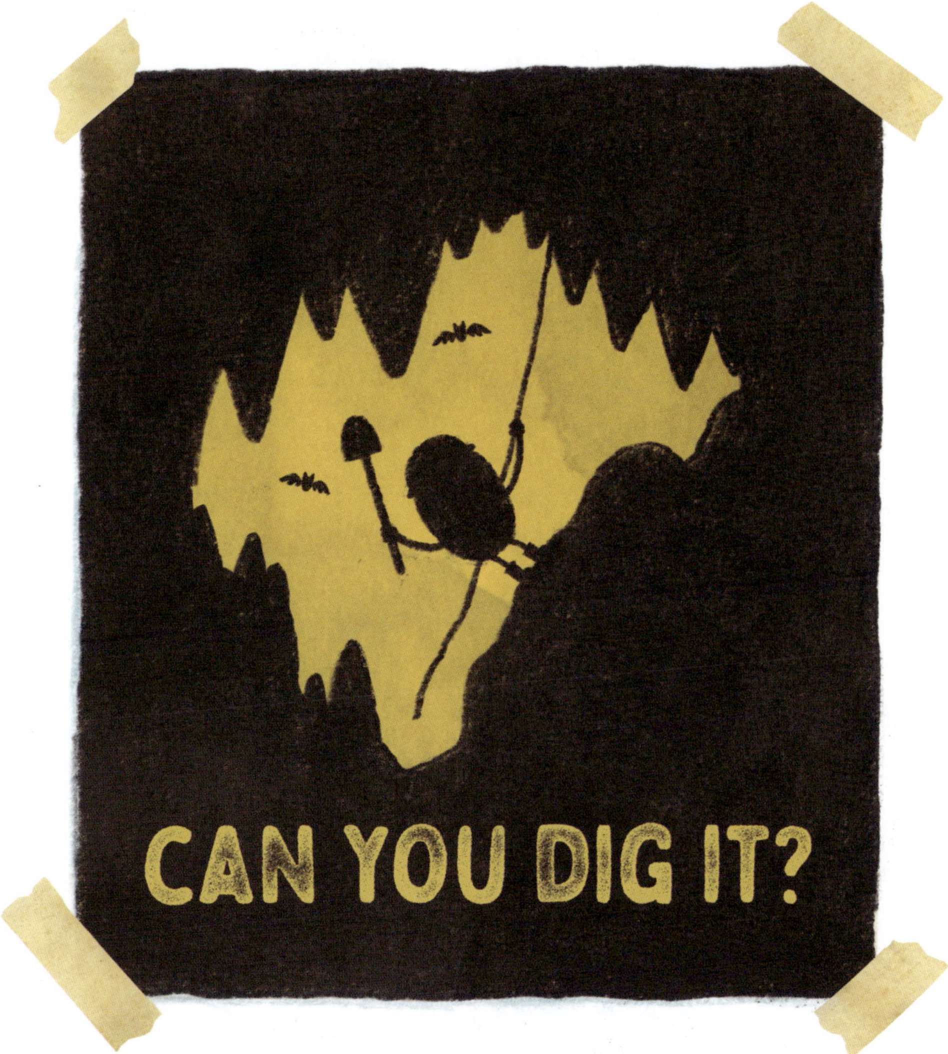
CAN YOU DIG IT?

Spudlunking is a little like that . . . except mutant potatoes dig their own caves to explore. Typically in mud and with the hope of unearthing treasures.

These are some of Rot's favorite finds:

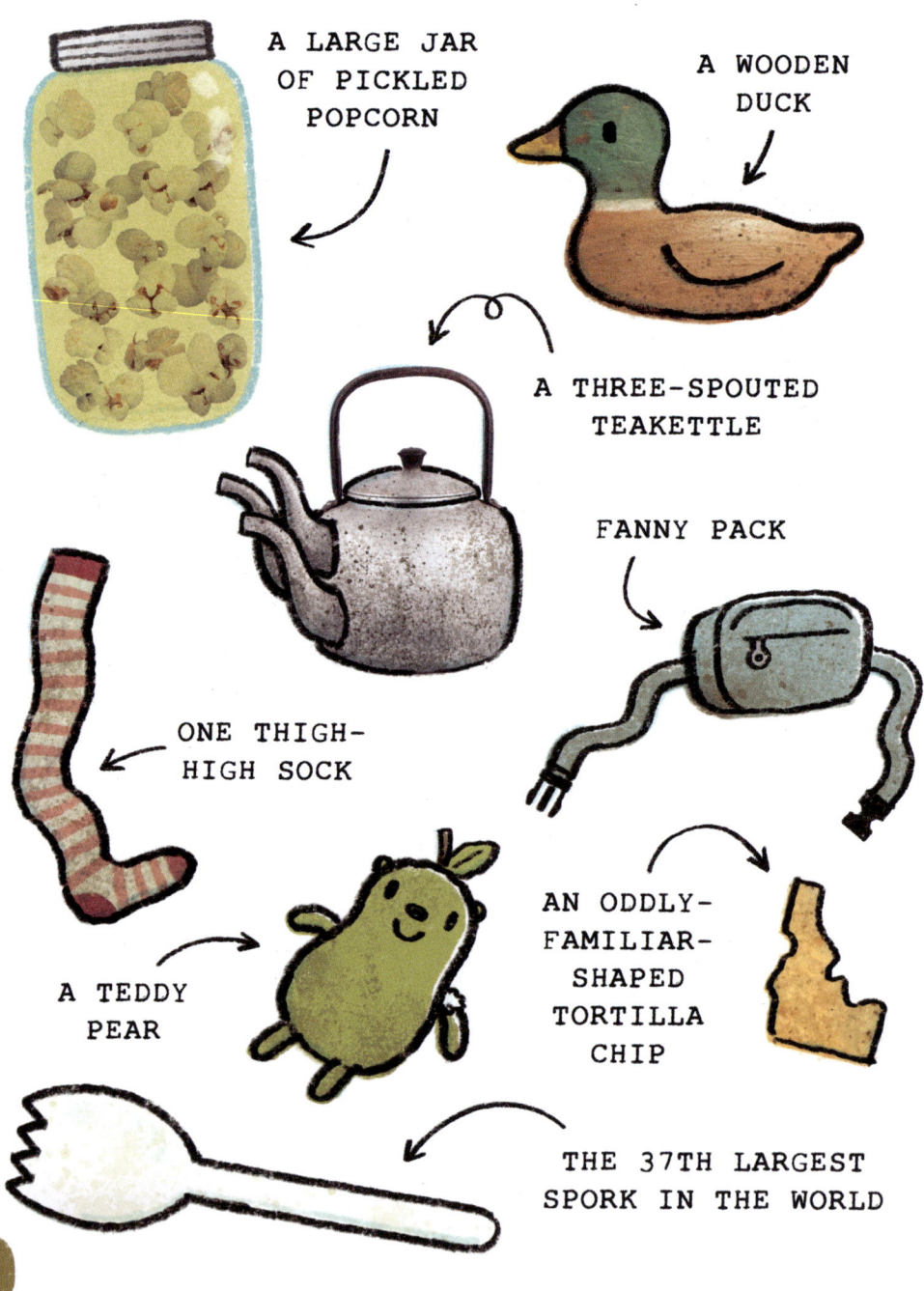

A LARGE JAR OF PICKLED POPCORN

A WOODEN DUCK

A THREE-SPOUTED TEAKETTLE

FANNY PACK

ONE THIGH-HIGH SOCK

A TEDDY PEAR

AN ODDLY-FAMILIAR-SHAPED TORTILLA CHIP

THE 37TH LARGEST SPORK IN THE WORLD

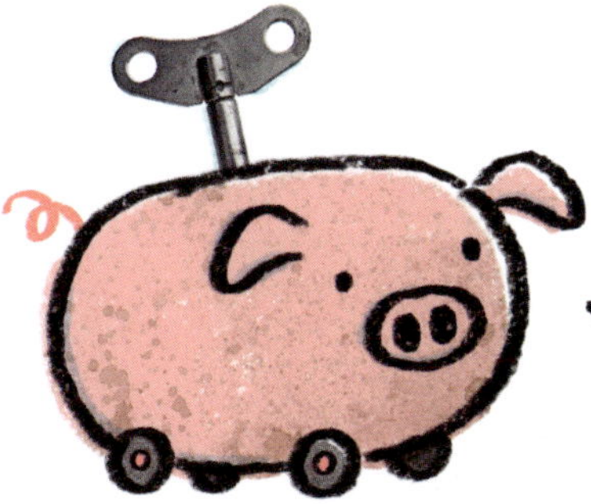

A WIND-UP PIG

A TWISTY STRAW

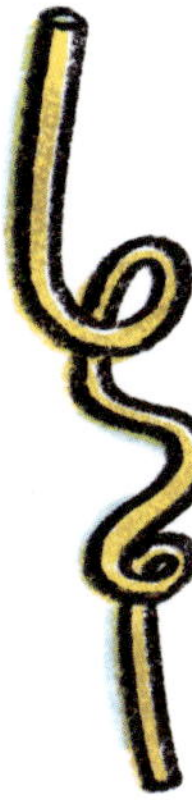

AN OLD MAILBOX

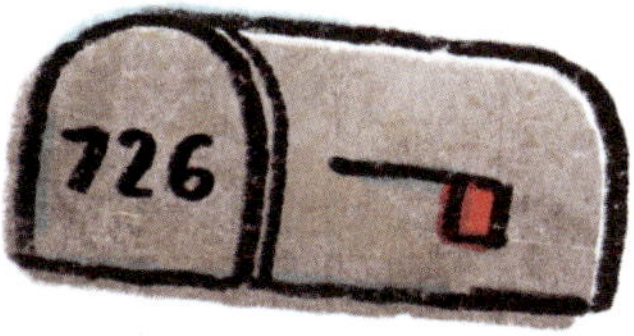
726

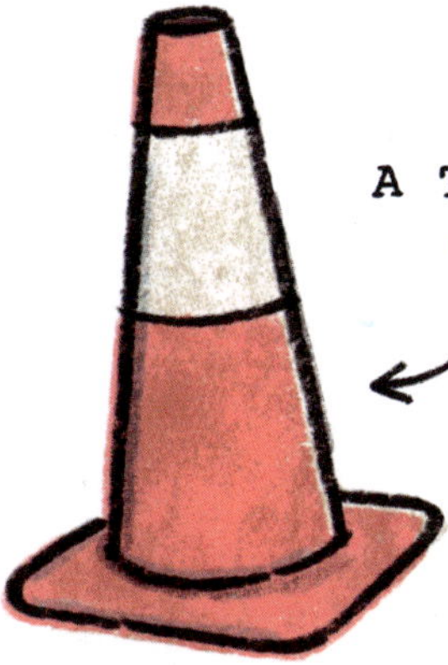

A TRAFFIC CONE

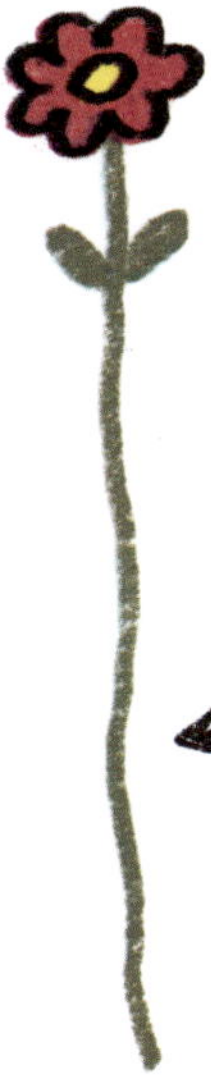

A FAKE FLOWER WITH AN UNUSUALLY LONG STEM

AN AIR FRESHENER

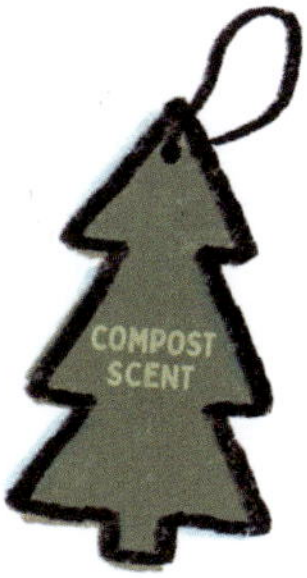
COMPOST SCENT

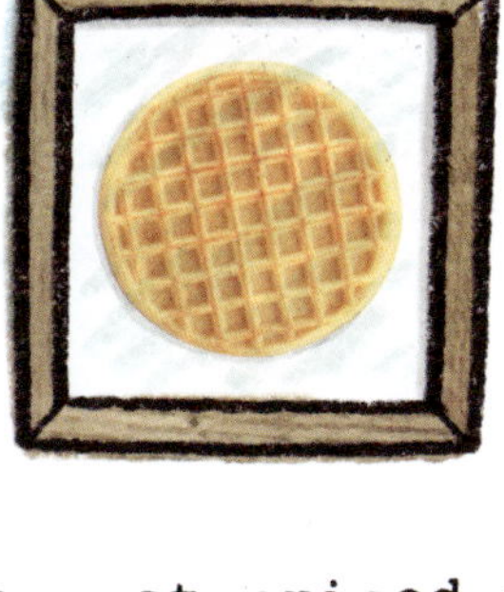

A FRAMED WAFFLE

But his most prized treasures are . . .

a hodgepodge of pots perfect for
Rot's cacti collection.

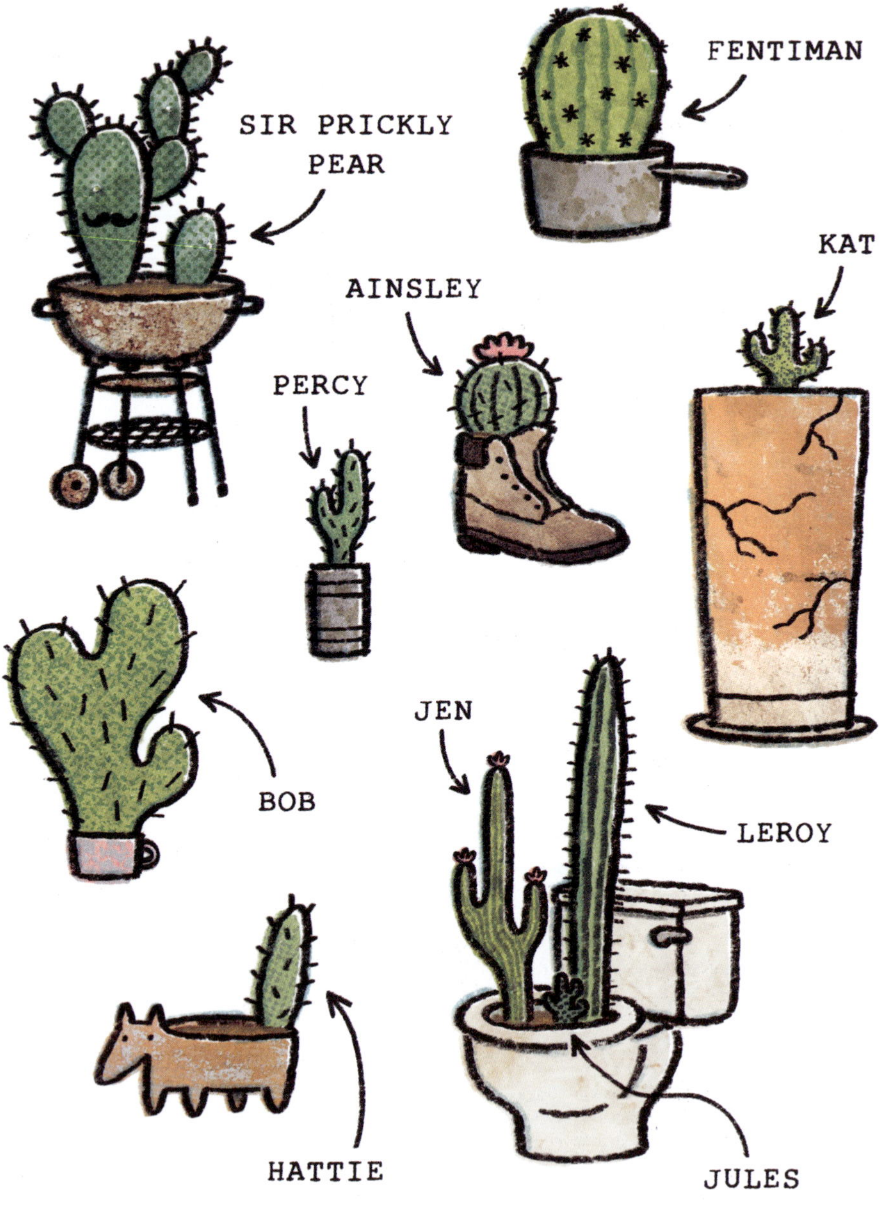
FENTIMAN
SIR PRICKLY PEAR
KAT
AINSLEY
PERCY
BOB
JEN
LEROY
HATTIE
JULES

Rot is almost ready to go dig up some new treasures. He just needs to find someone to join him first. Spudlunking is best with a buddy.

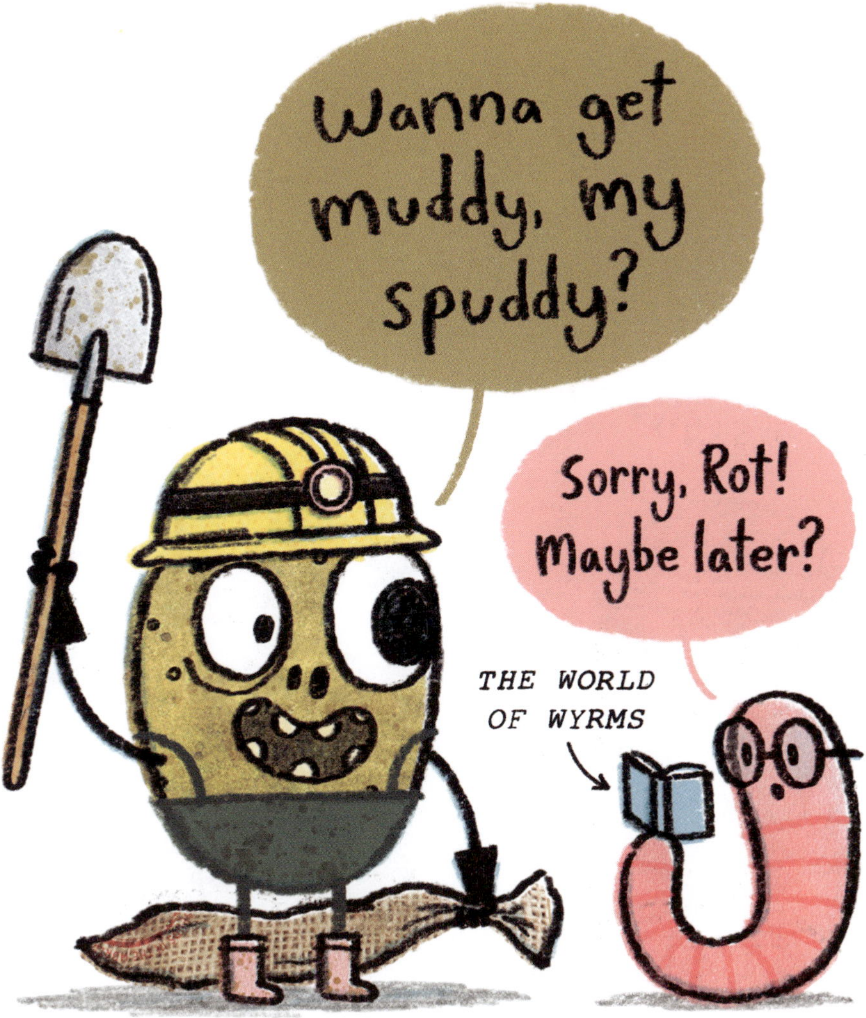
Wanna get muddy, my spuddy?
Sorry, Rot! Maybe later?
THE WORLD OF WYRMS

But his best bud, Worm, is too engrossed in an exciting book.

And Rot's little sister, Tot, is too busy trying out a new trick.

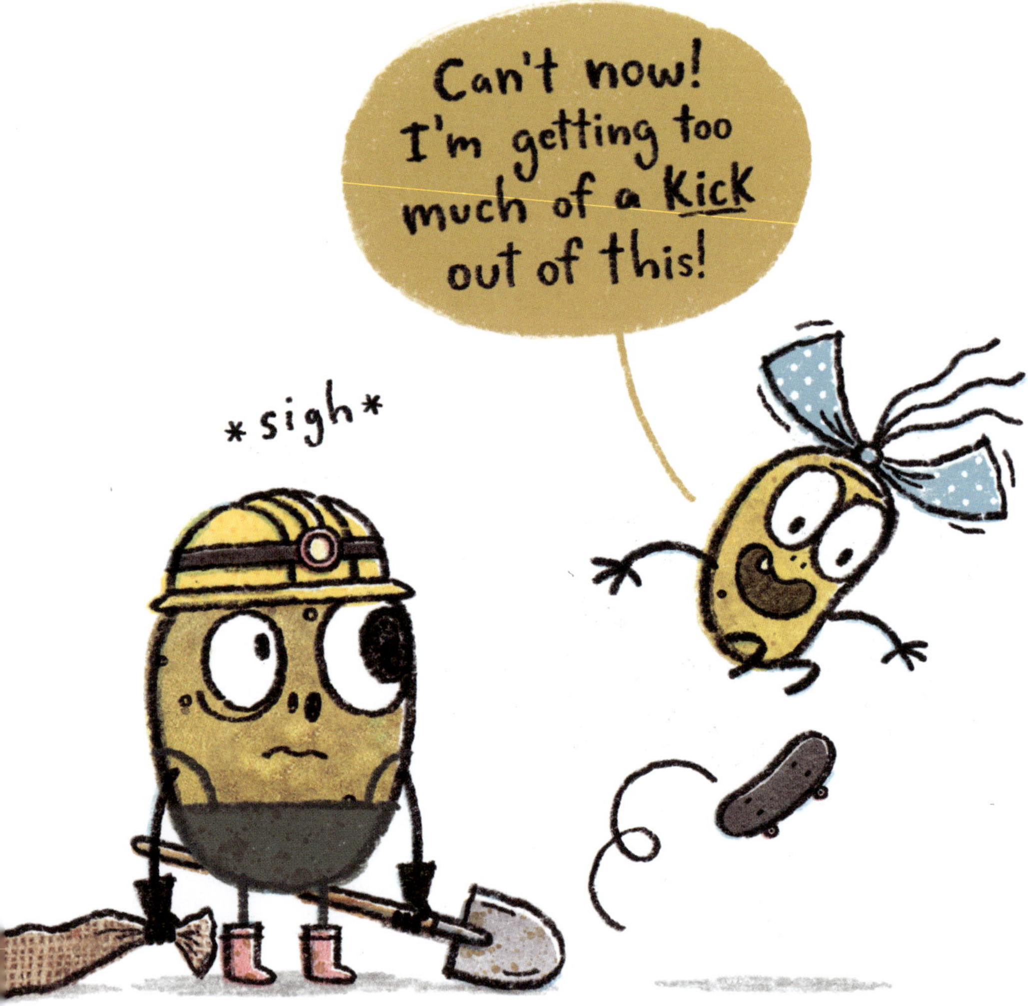
Can't now! I'm getting too much of a Kick out of this!
sigh

As for Rot's big brother, Snot . . .

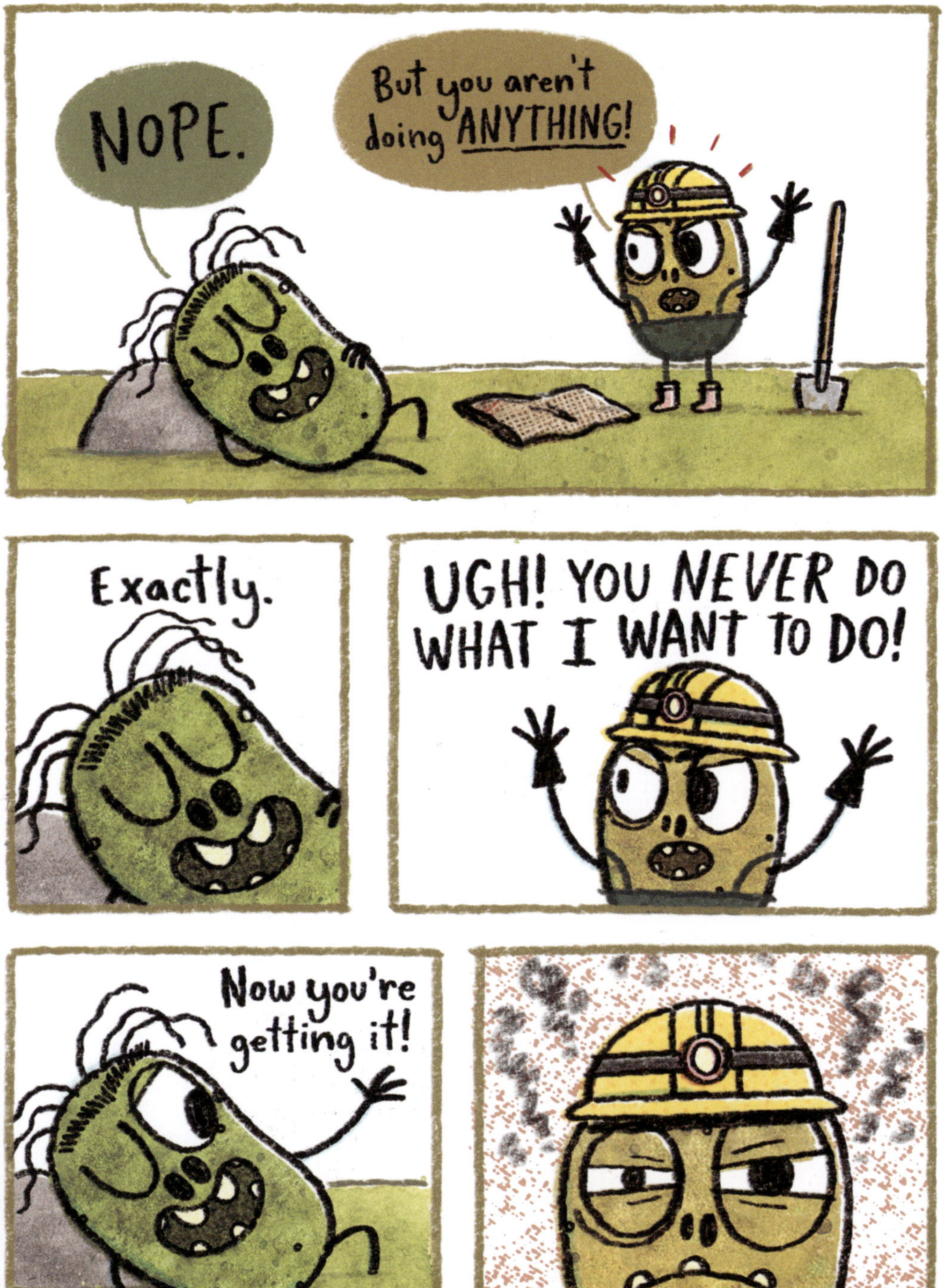
NOPE.
But you aren't doing ANYTHING!
Exactly.
UGH! YOU NEVER DO WHAT I WANT TO DO!
Now you're getting it!

Unable to find a spuddy, Rot decides to make it a solo spudlunk. He's now determined to find something extra special, a treasure like no other!

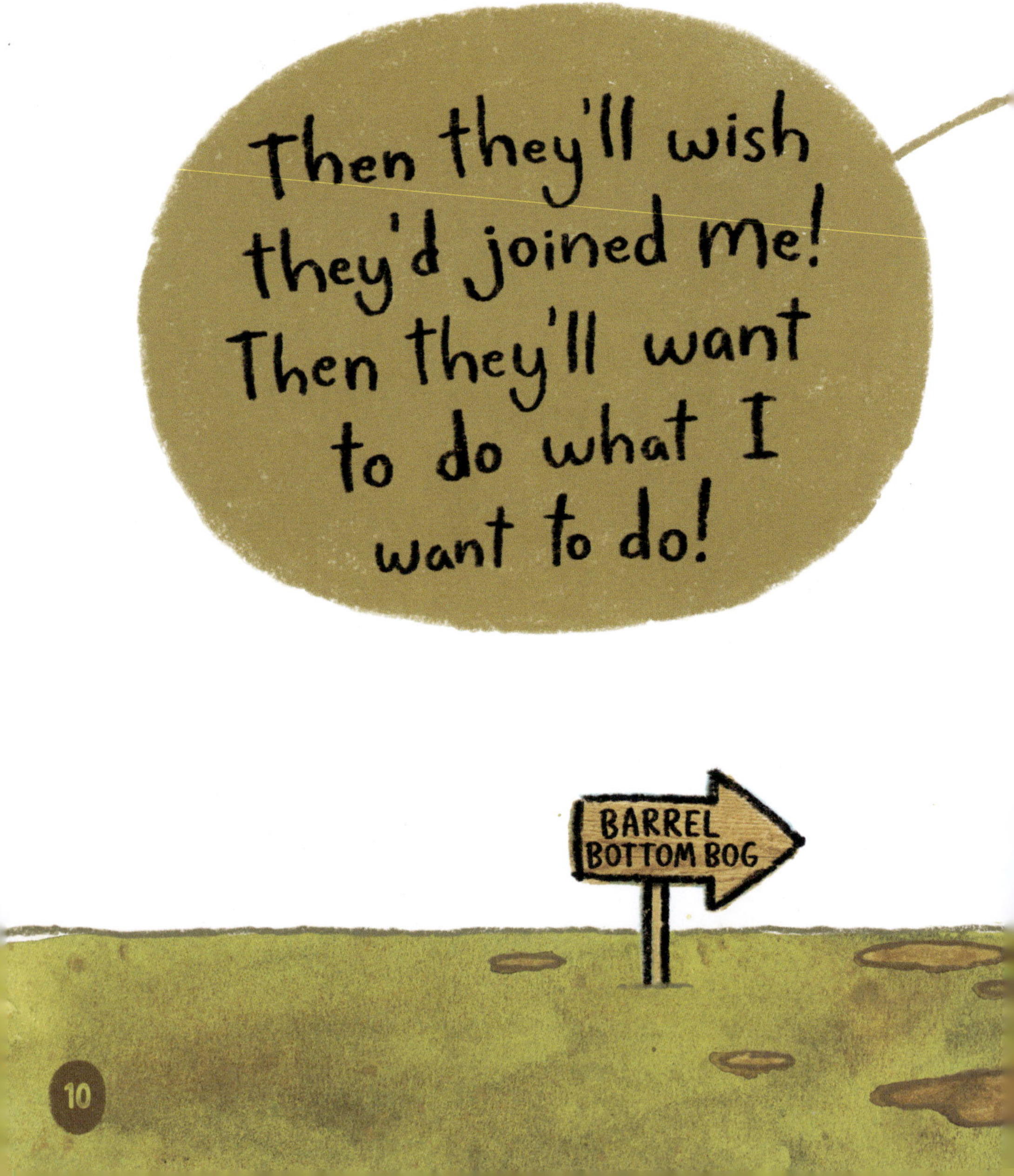
Then they'll wish they'd joined me! Then they'll want to do what I want to do!
BARREL BOTTOM BOG

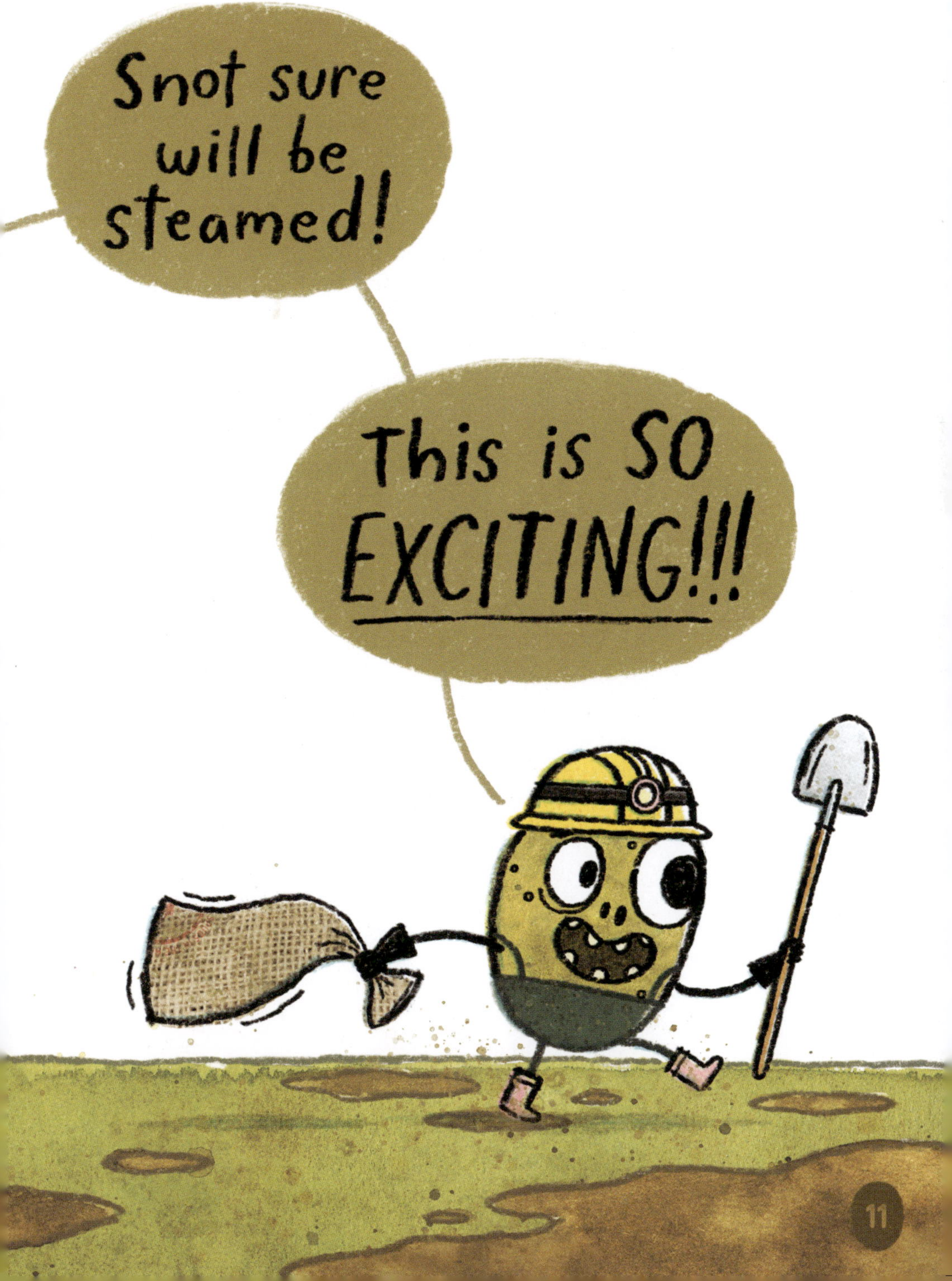
Snot sure will be steamed!
This is SO EXCITING!!!

CHAPTER 2
HOLEY MOLEY

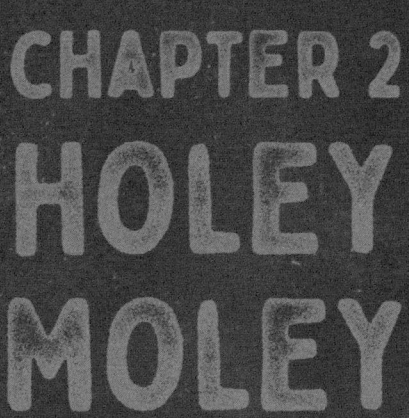

Rot starts digging. He digs and digs and digs! As he digs he sings a song.

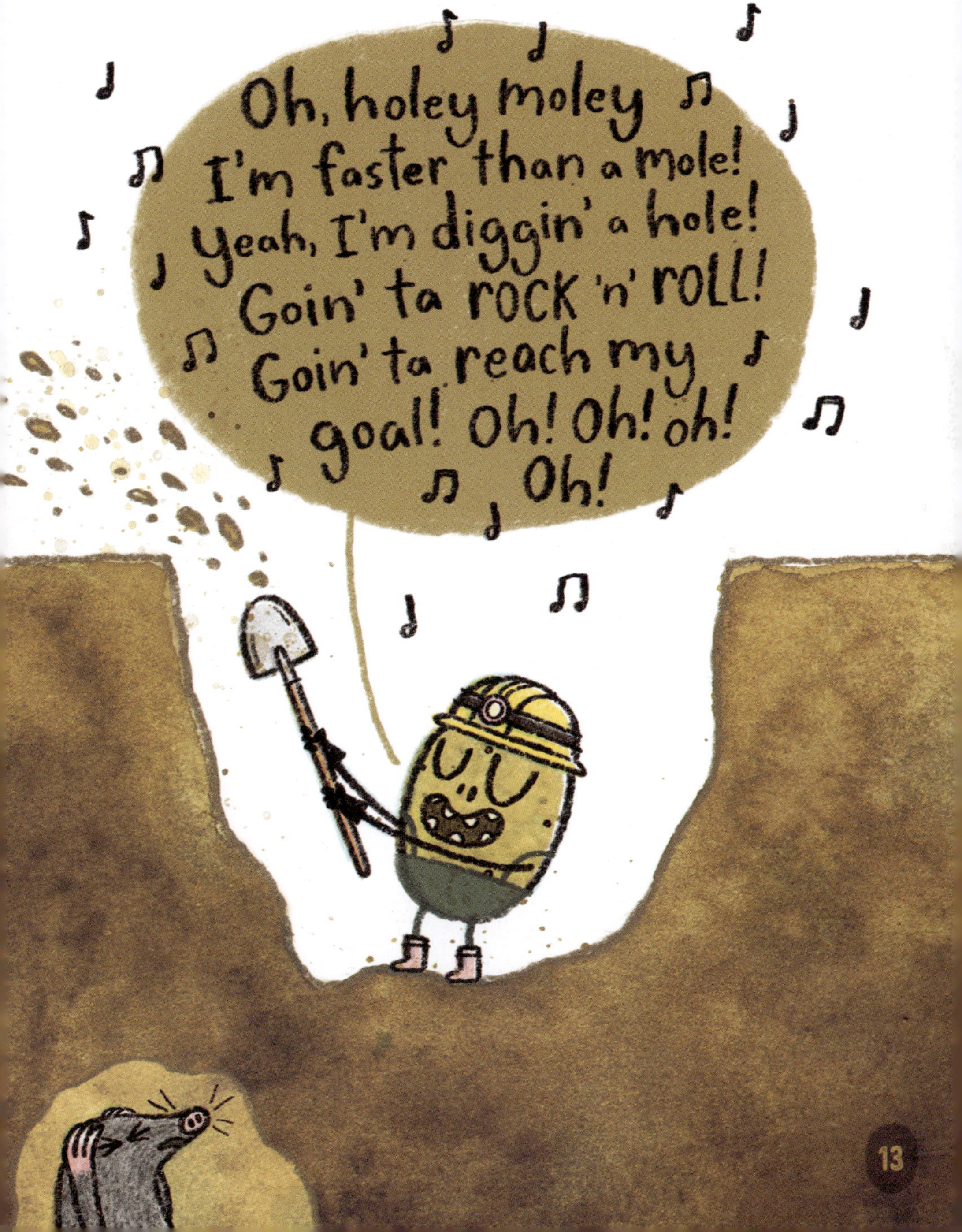
Oh, holey moley I'm faster than a mole! Yeah, I'm diggin' a hole! Goin' ta ROCK 'n' ROLL! Goin' ta reach my goal! Oh! Oh! oh! Oh!

And as Rot sings he dreams . . .

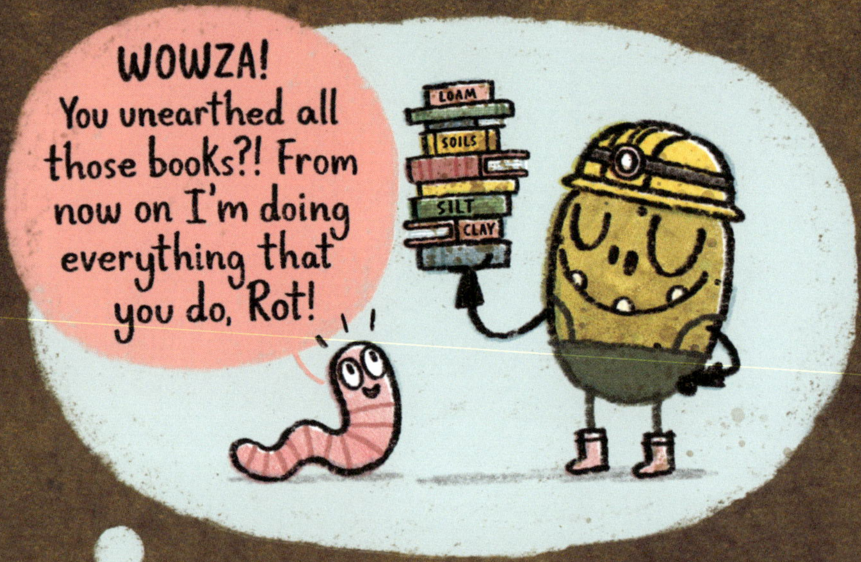
WOWZA! You unearthed all those books?! From now on I'm doing everything that you do, Rot!
LOAM
SOILS
SILT
CLAY

and dreams . . .

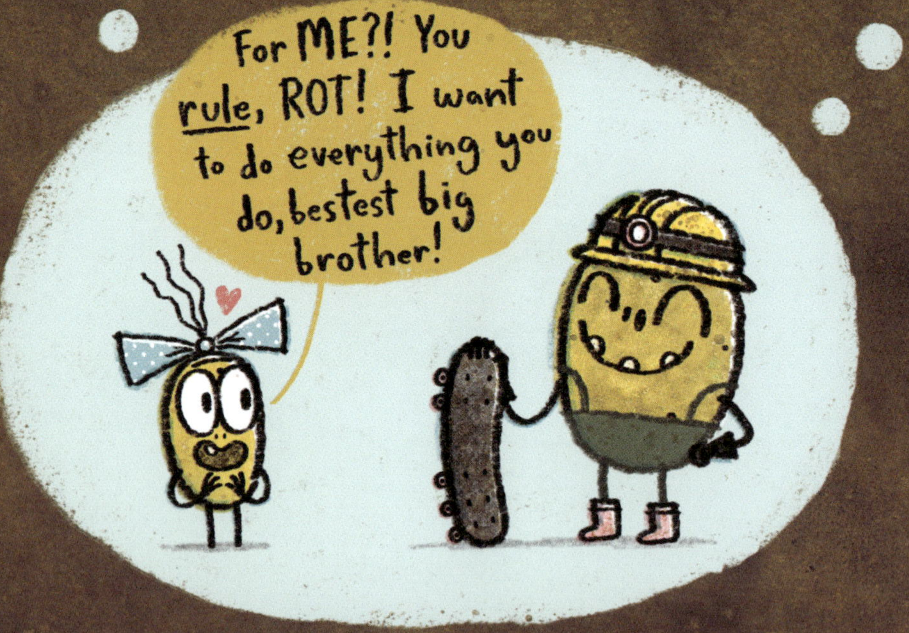
For ME?! You rule, ROT! I want to do everything you do, bestest big brother!

and dreams . . .

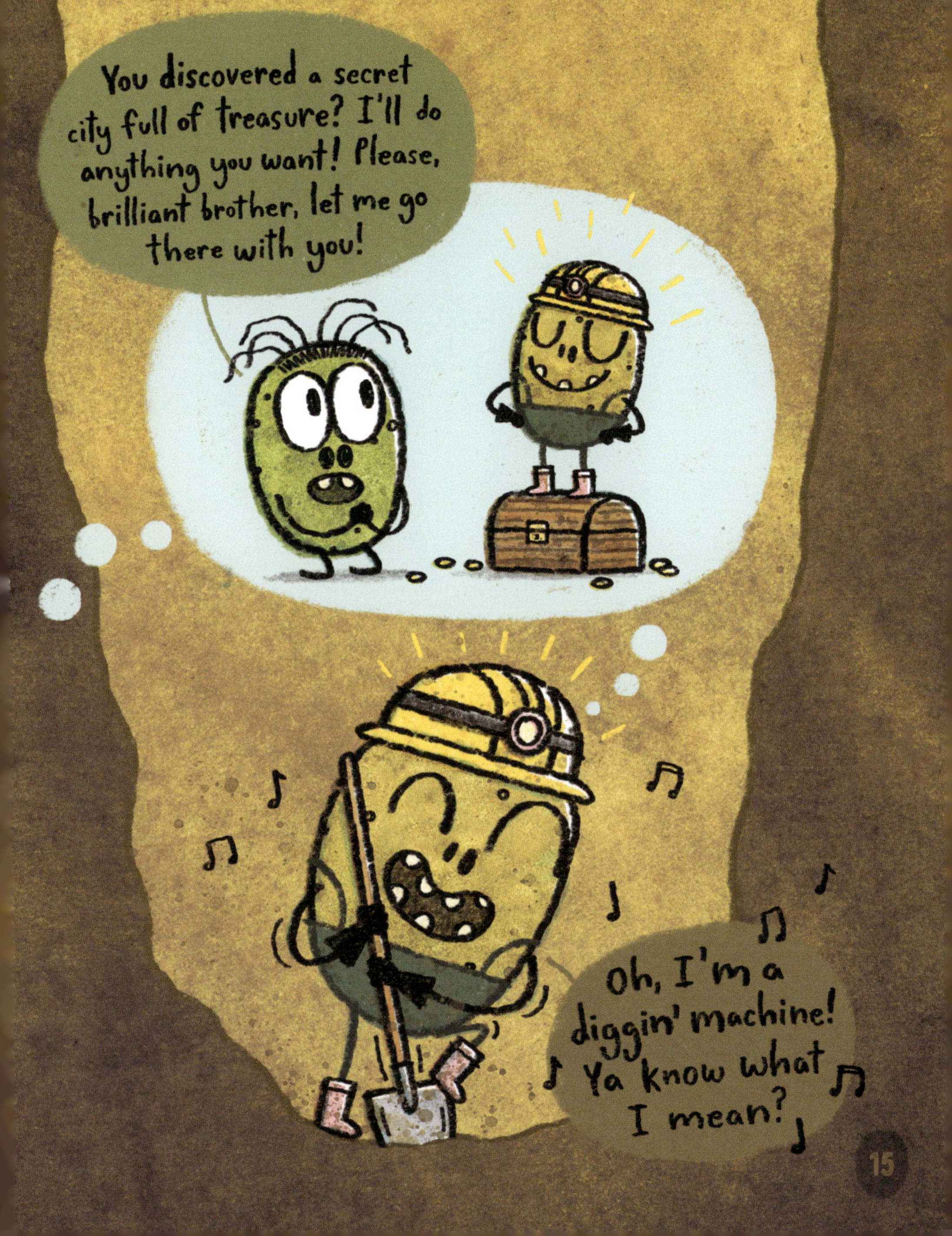

You discovered a secret city full of treasure? I'll do anything you want! Please, brilliant brother, let me go there with you!
Oh, I'm a diggin' machine! Ya know what I mean?

But it seems Rot's dreams won't become reality. He has reached new depths! Gone where no spuddy has spudlunked before! But . . . he still hasn't found a single thing.

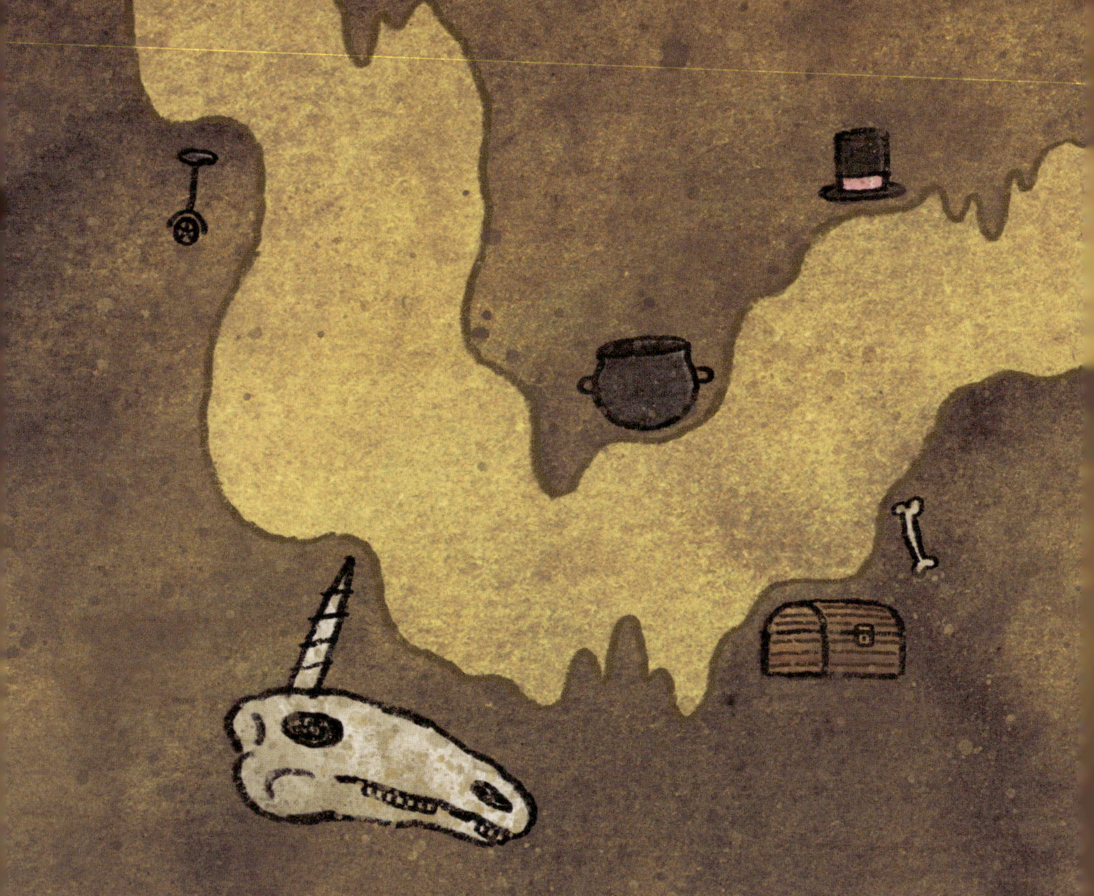

Has Rot reached rock bottom?
Has his spudlunking quest come to an end?

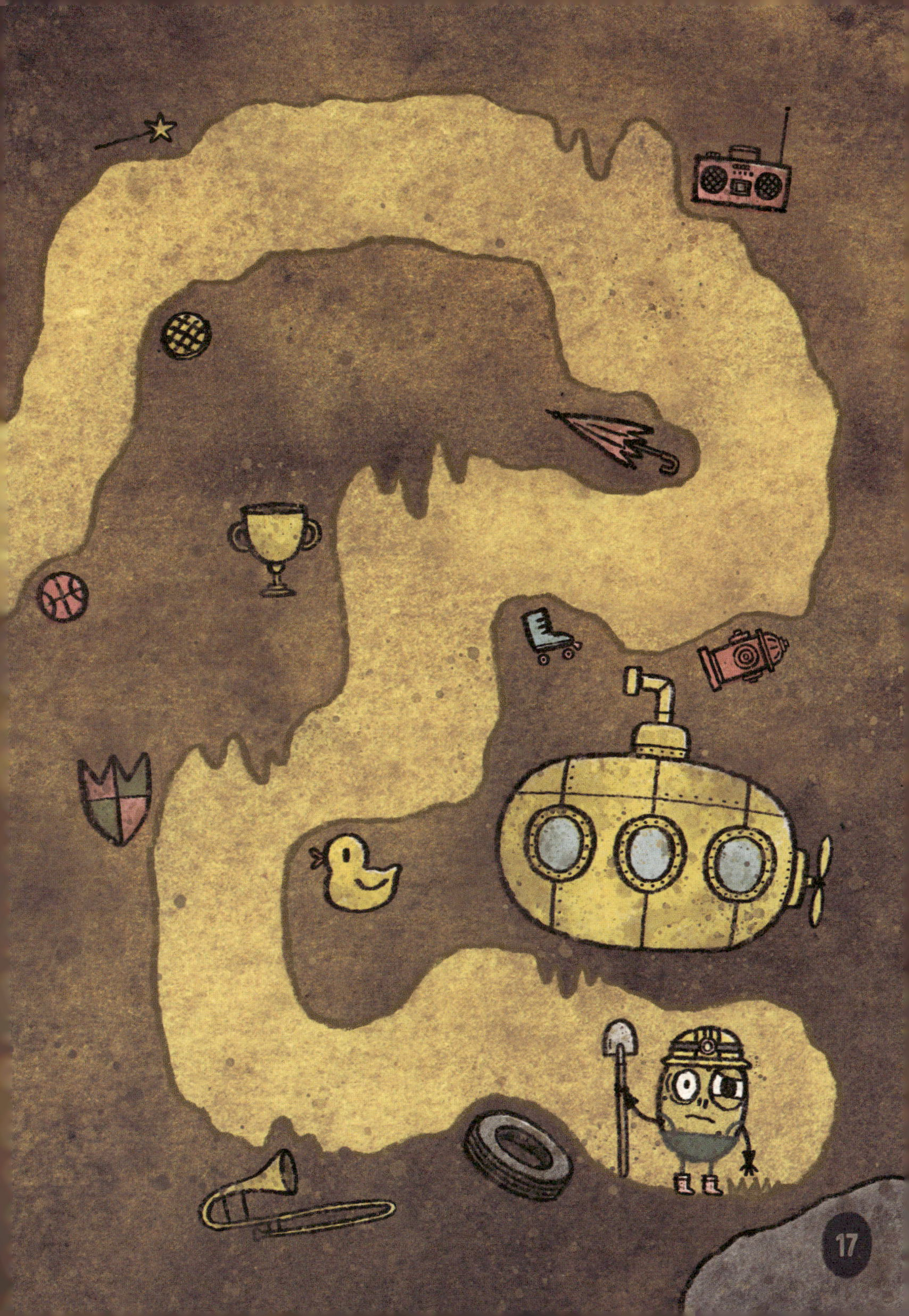

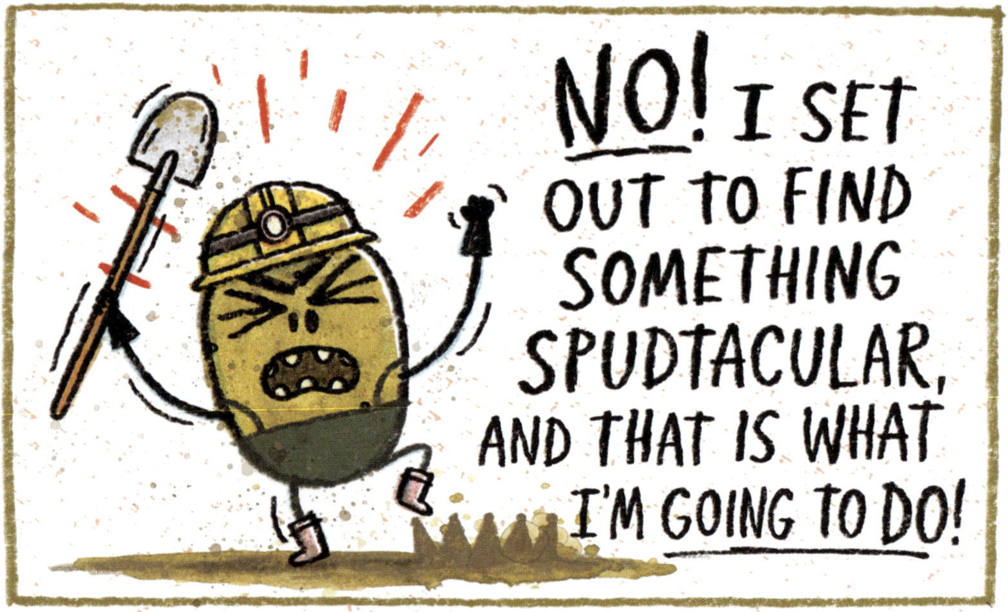
NO! I SET OUT TO FIND SOMETHING SPUDTACULAR, AND THAT IS WHAT I'M GOING TO DO!

And that's when he stumbles upon it . . .
or rather stomps upon it.

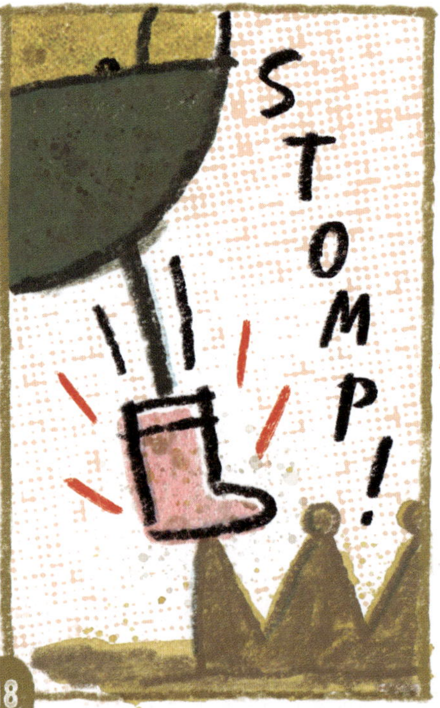
STOMP!

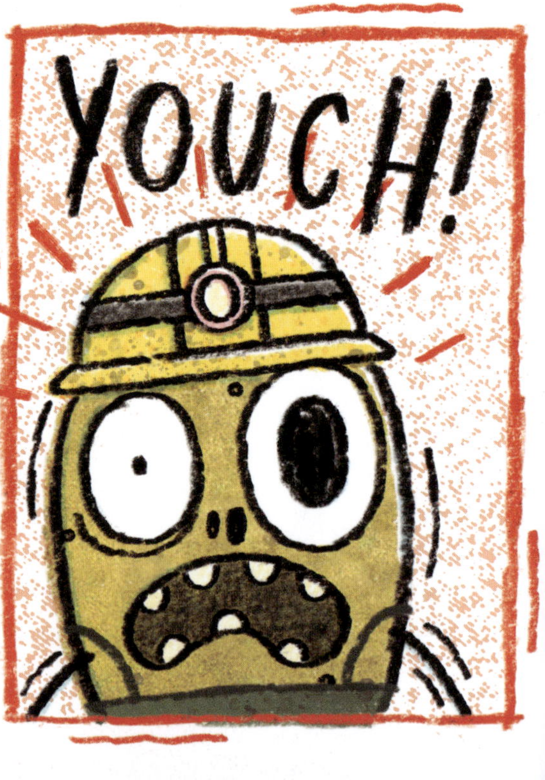
YOUCH!

It is a crusty, musty, and more than dusty crown.

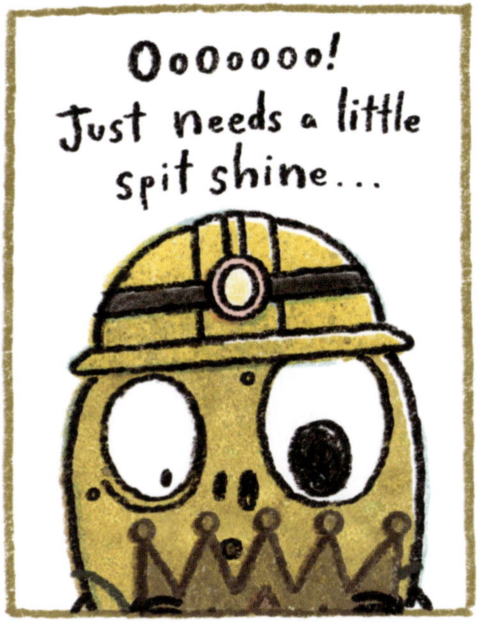
Ooooooo!
Just needs a little
spit shine...

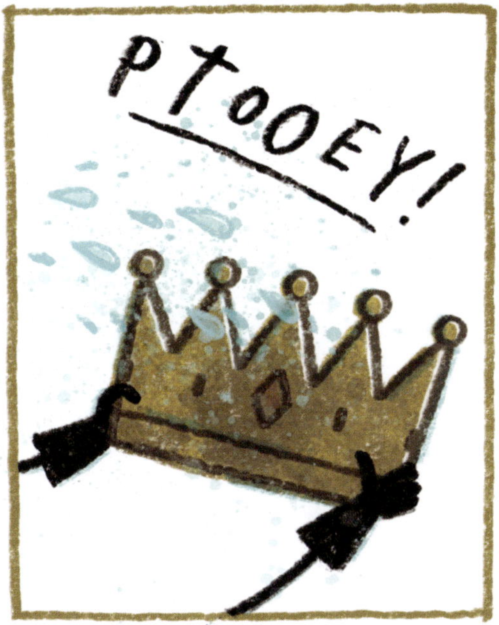
PTOOEY!

Actually it takes a lot of spit (and some serious scrubbing) to make that crown shine, but before long it looks divine!

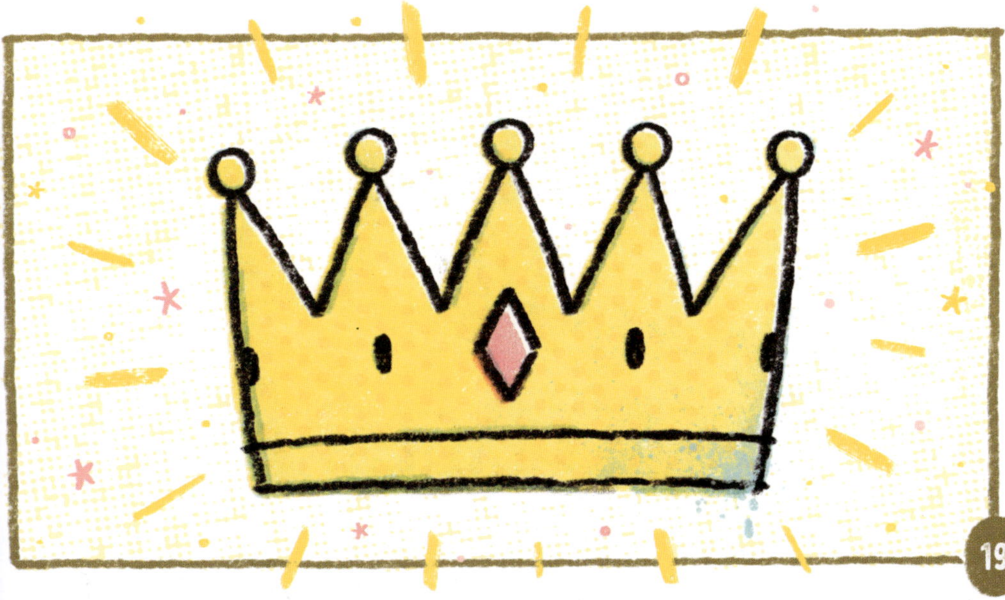

Rot places the crown upon his head and is filled with a strange and fantastic feeling. He feels somehow stronger. He feels important! He feels powerful. He feels like he can do anything he wants to do. He feels like . . . a KING! Like the . . .

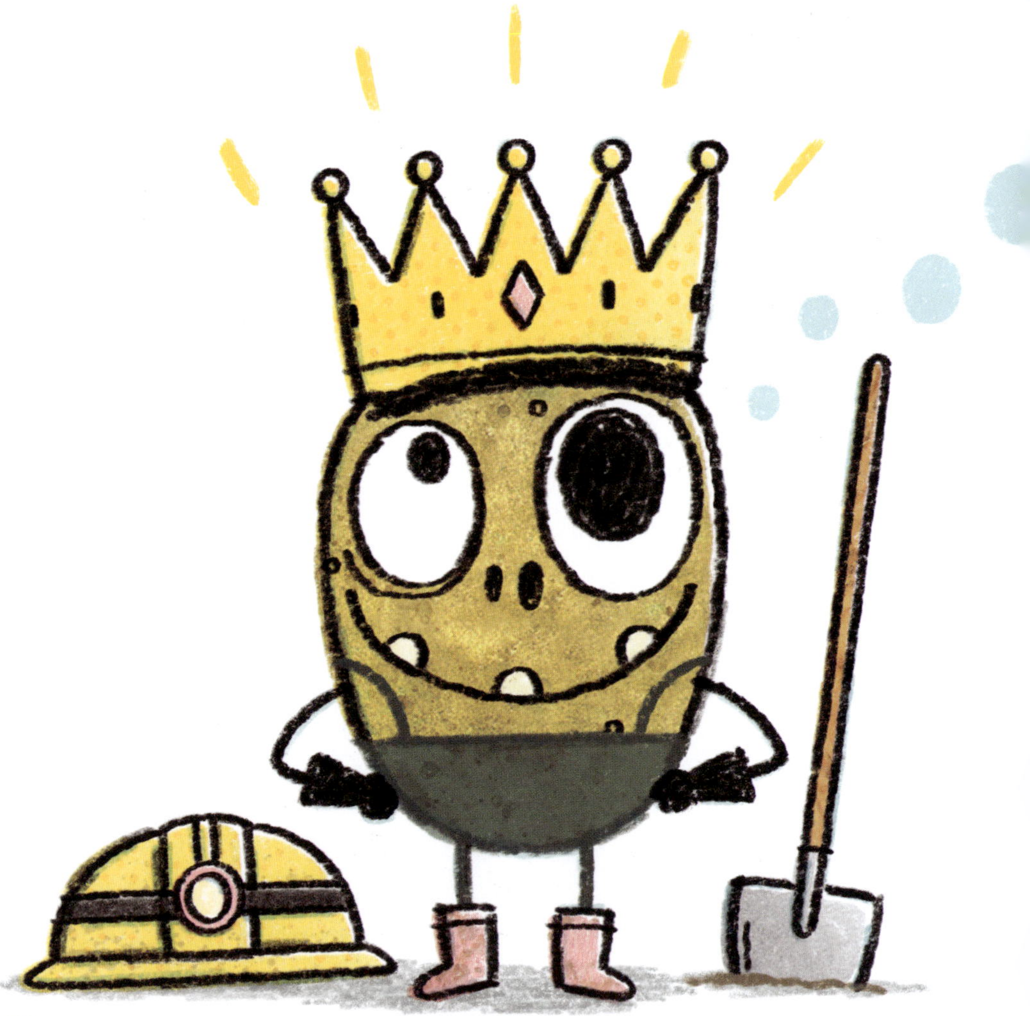

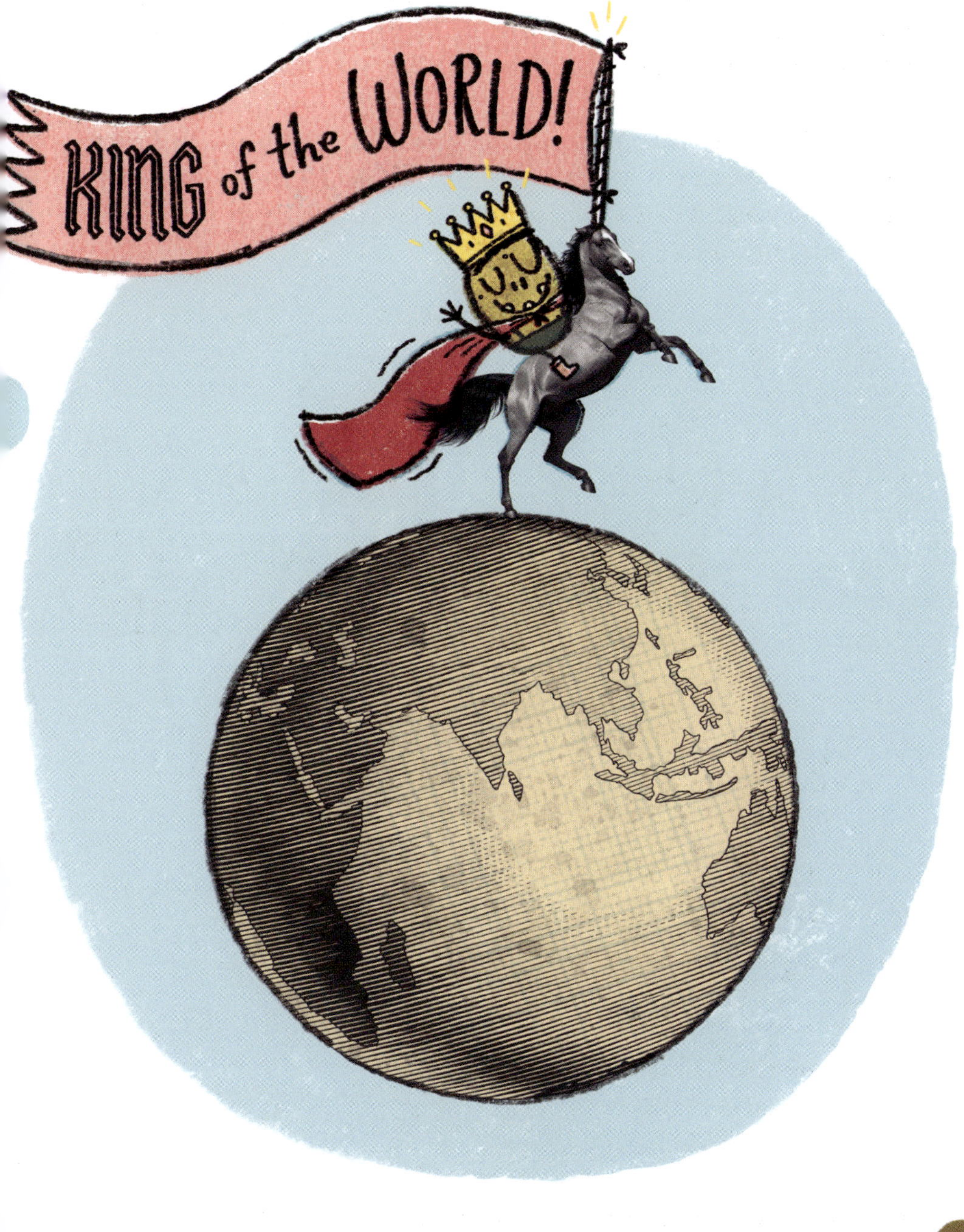
KING of the WORLD!

But another had felt like the King of the World before Rot. Unbeknownst to Rot (fancy way of saying "he didn't have a clue"), the crown he'd unearthed was one of legend.

Long before mutant potatoes dug caves in the muds of Barrel Bottom Bog, the Pickle People once lived dill-lightful lives there, relishing every moment.

All was brine, er, fine until one day . . .

the Sour One came, wearing that legendary crown, and put the Pickle People under his spell. He made them name him the King of the Pickle Patch.

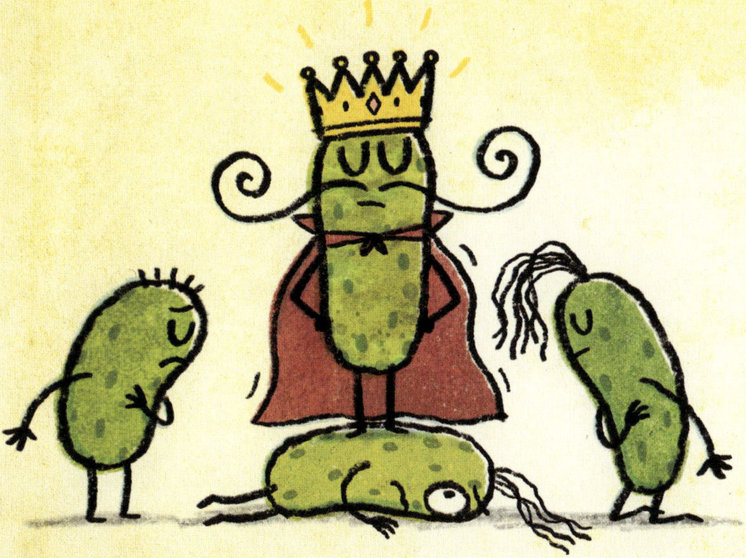

But the Sour One was a pickle gone bad, and he was not content to rule just the Pickle People. He wanted the world.

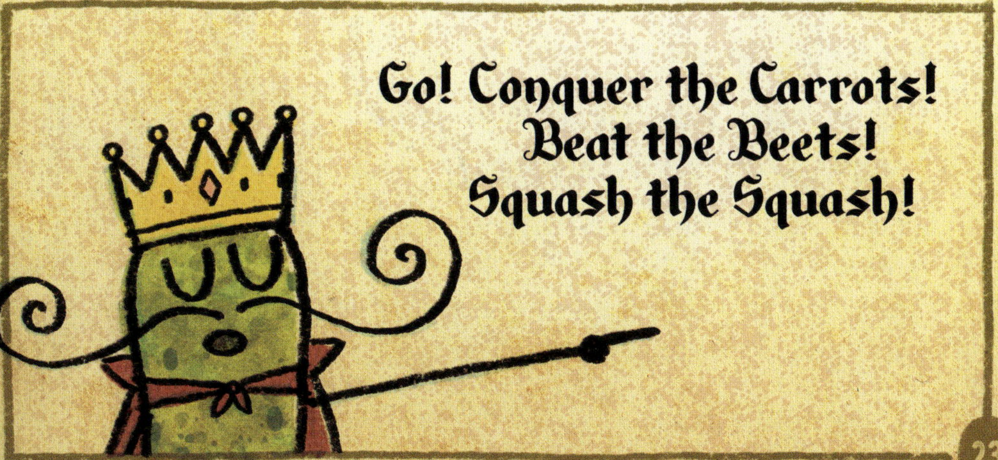
Go! Conquer the Carrots!
Beat the Beets!
Squash the Squash!

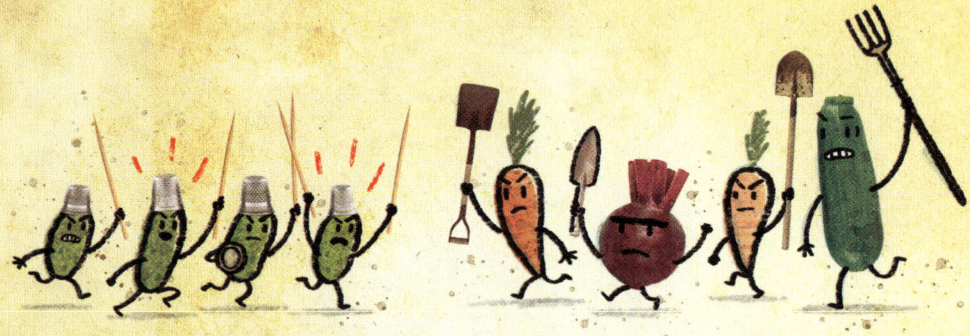

In the end the Sour One was defeated. But before he fell, he vowed that one day he would return to rule them all.

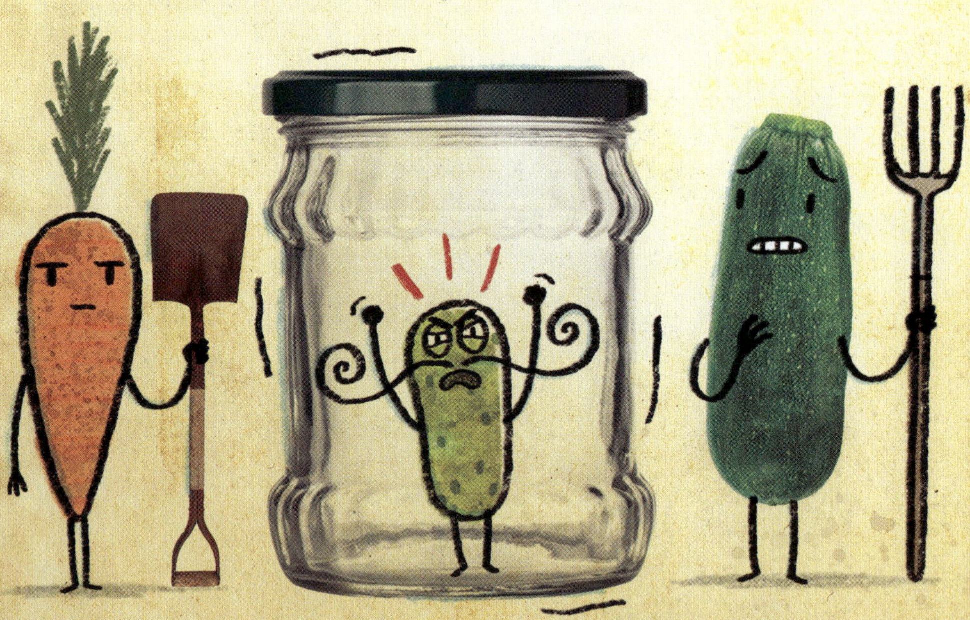

It is said that he put all his power into his crown. A crown that went missing.

Many searched for it. Rumor has it that this is how spudlunking started. But the crown was never found . . . until now.

CHAPTER 3
KING ME!

Rot is eager to show everyone his magnificent crown, but he doesn't run home. No, he struts! He sashays! He promenades! Rot gets so caught up in walking in a dignified and kingly way that he doesn't spot the snake. . . .

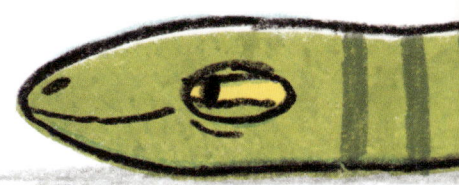

Typically a snake wouldn't eat a potato, but this snake doesn't have the best eyesight. To the snake, Rot looks like a large, delicious egg. But Rot doesn't panic. In his most regal voice he simply commands the snake to . . .

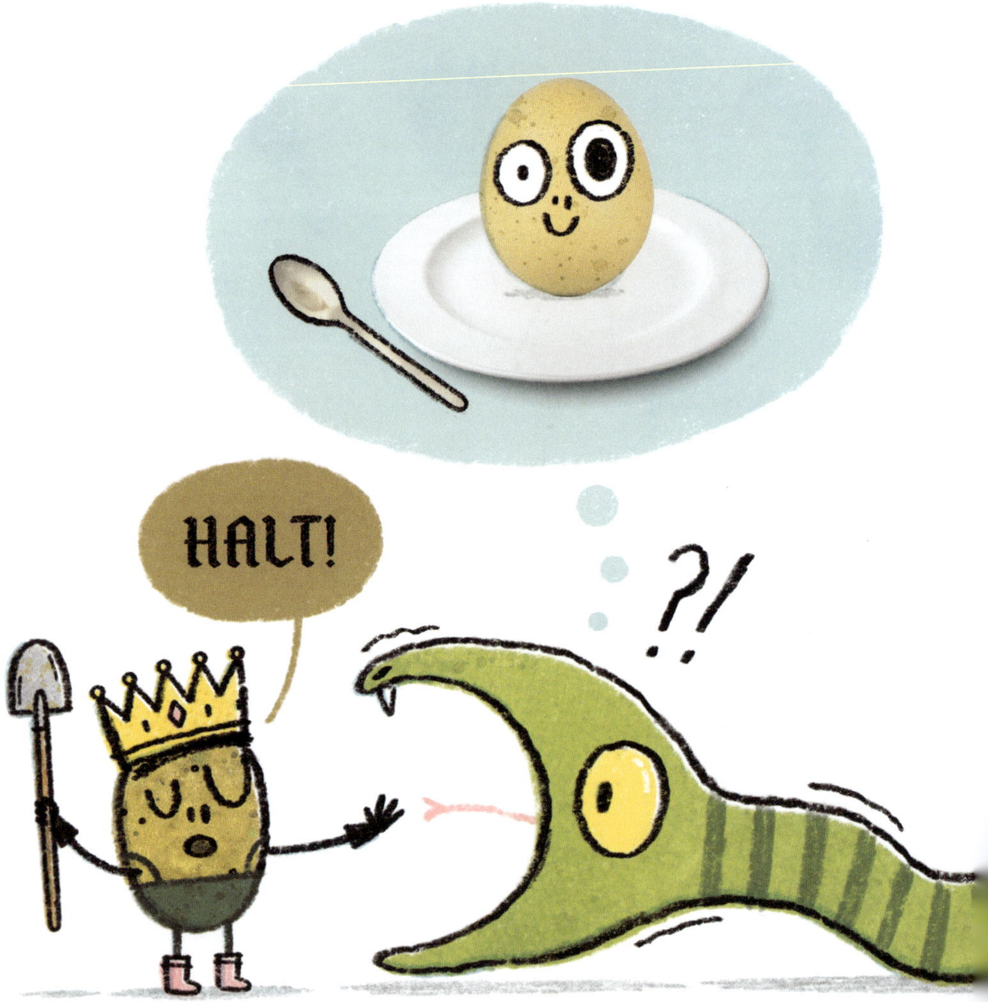
HALT!
?!

And much to the snake's surprise she does.

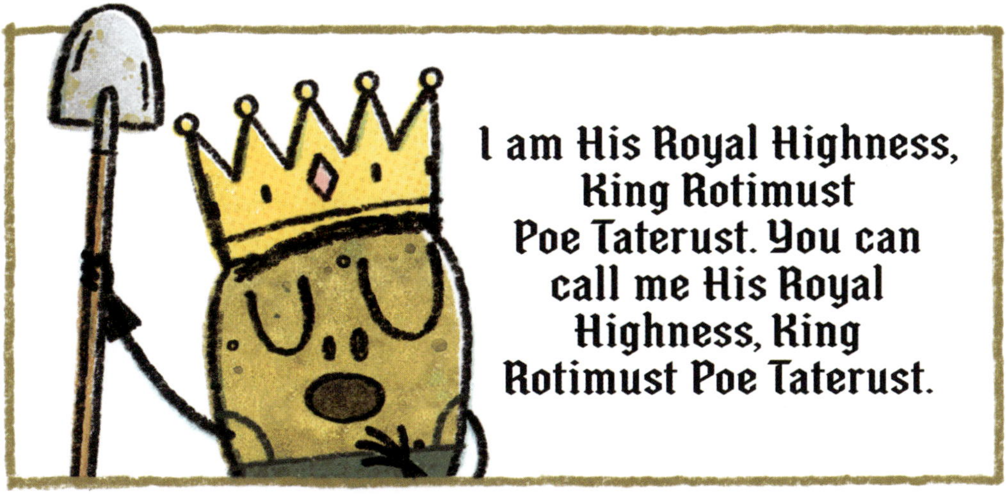
I am His Royal Highness, King Rotimust Poe Taterust. You can call me His Royal Highness, King Rotimust Poe Taterust.

After this proclamation (fancy way of saying he said something greatly important), Rot steps upon the snake's back.

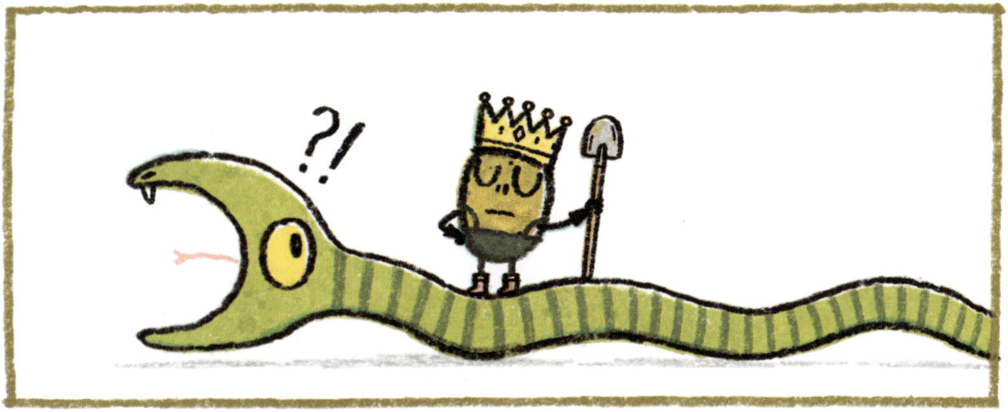
?!

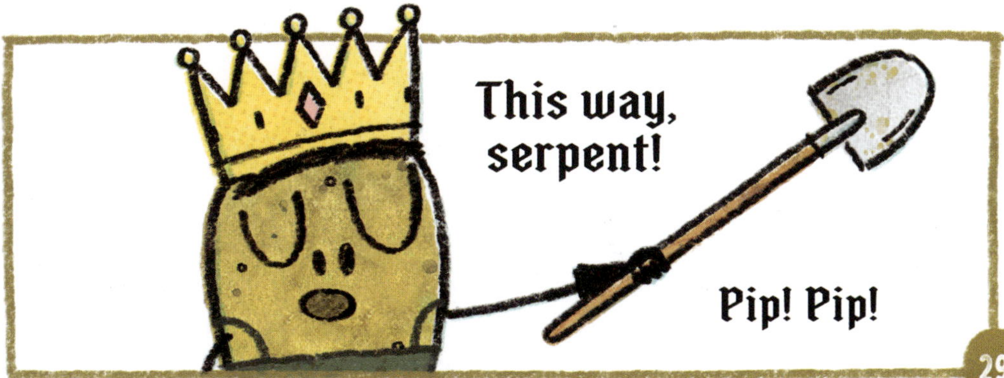
This way, serpent!
Pip! Pip!

Nearing home, Rot spies Snot. He awakens his big brother from a lovely six-and-a-half-hour nap with a startling sight.

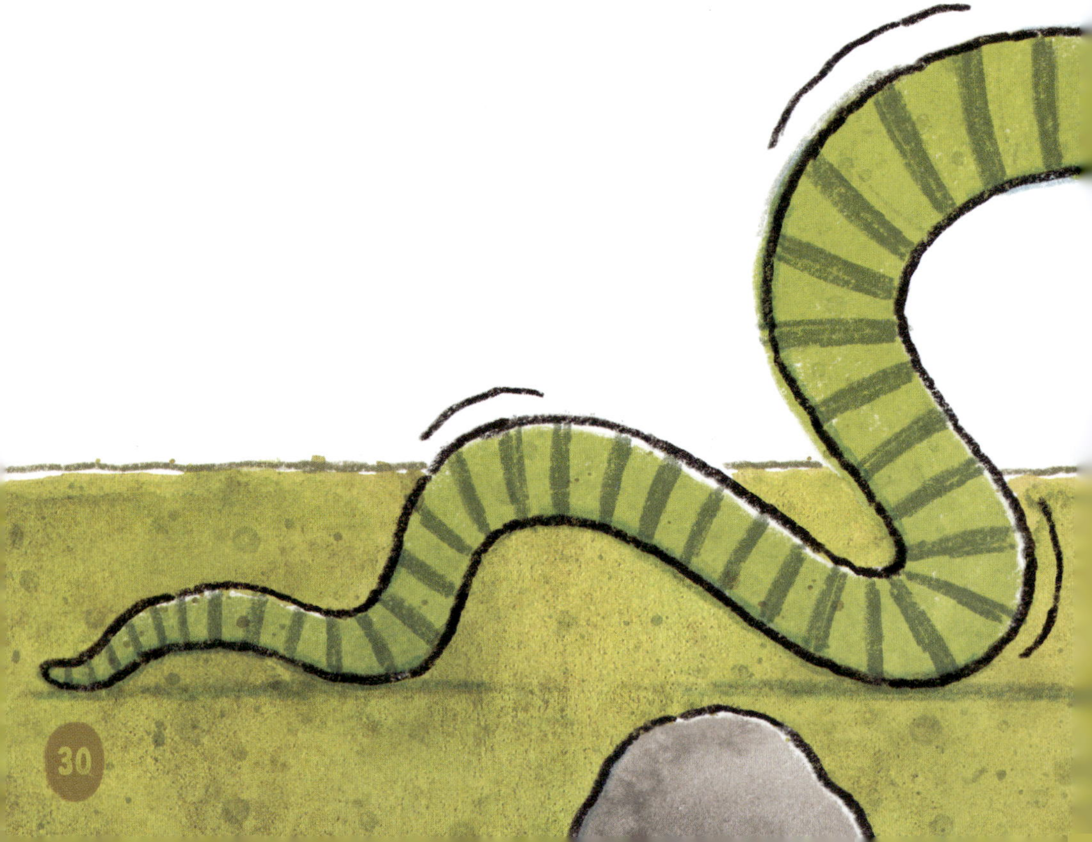

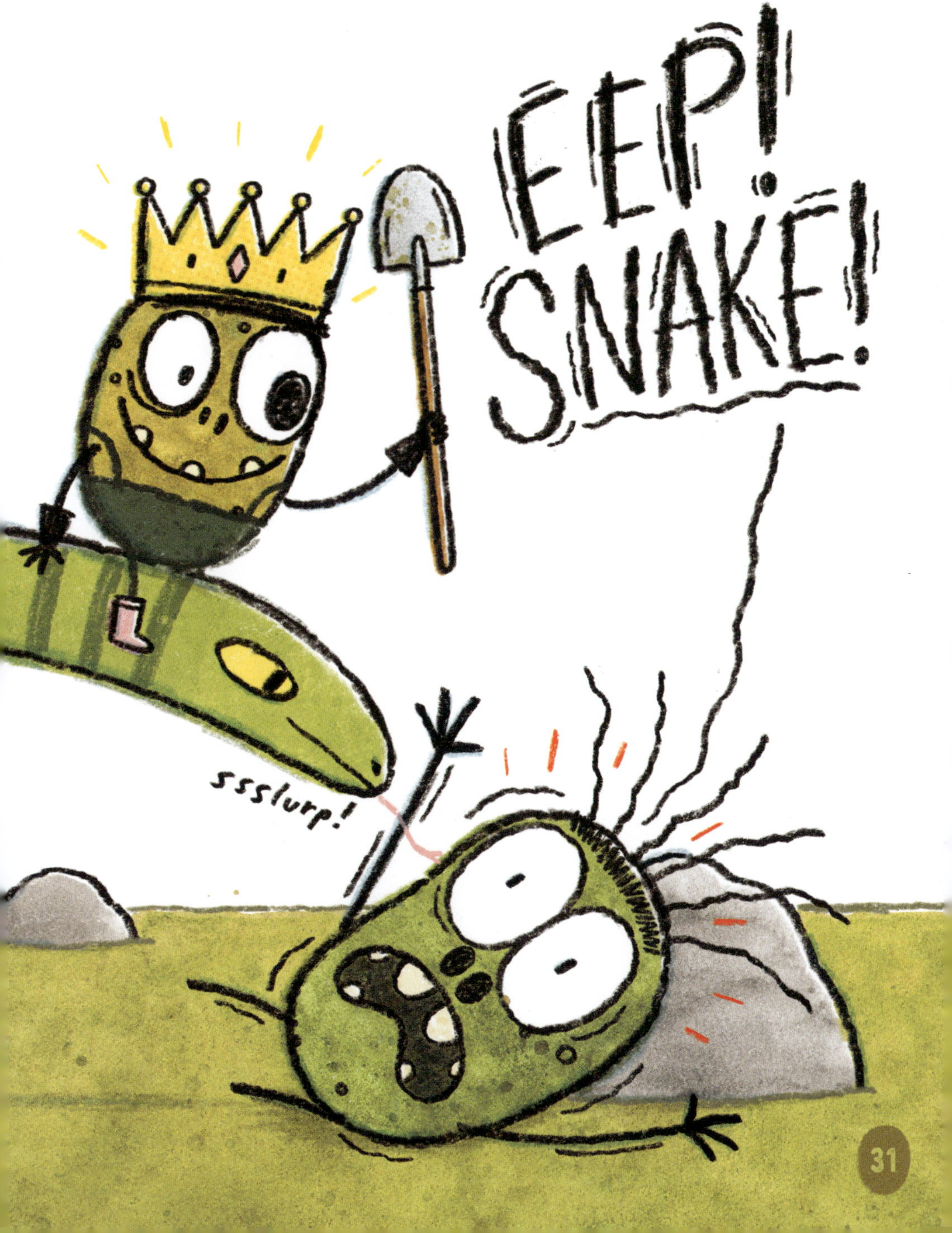
EEP! SNAKE!
ssslurp!

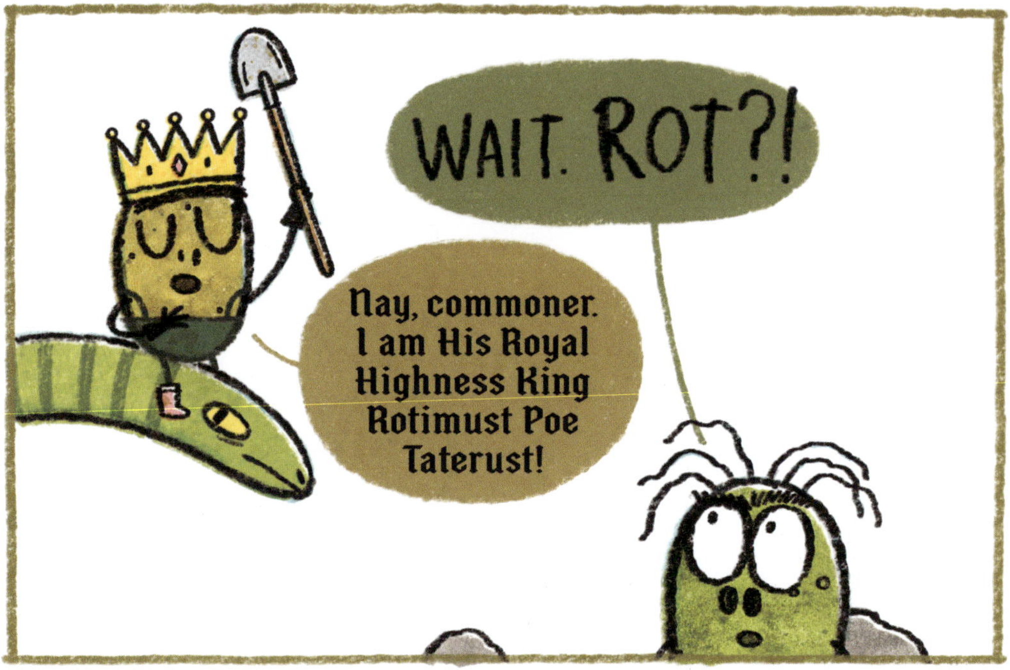
WAIT. ROT?!
Nay, commoner. I am His Royal Highness King Rotimust Poe Taterust!

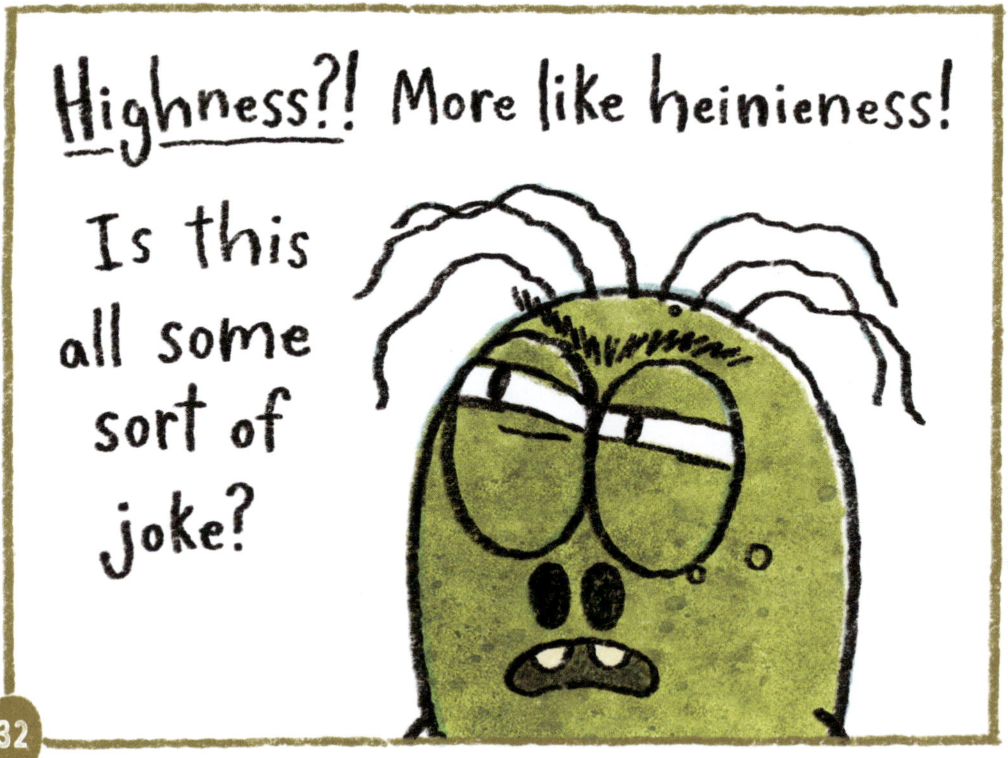
Highness?! More like heinieness!
Is this all some sort of joke?

Rot considers ordering the snake to eat Snot for being such a snot. But that wouldn't be a very nice thing to do. Besides, something more fitting comes to mind.

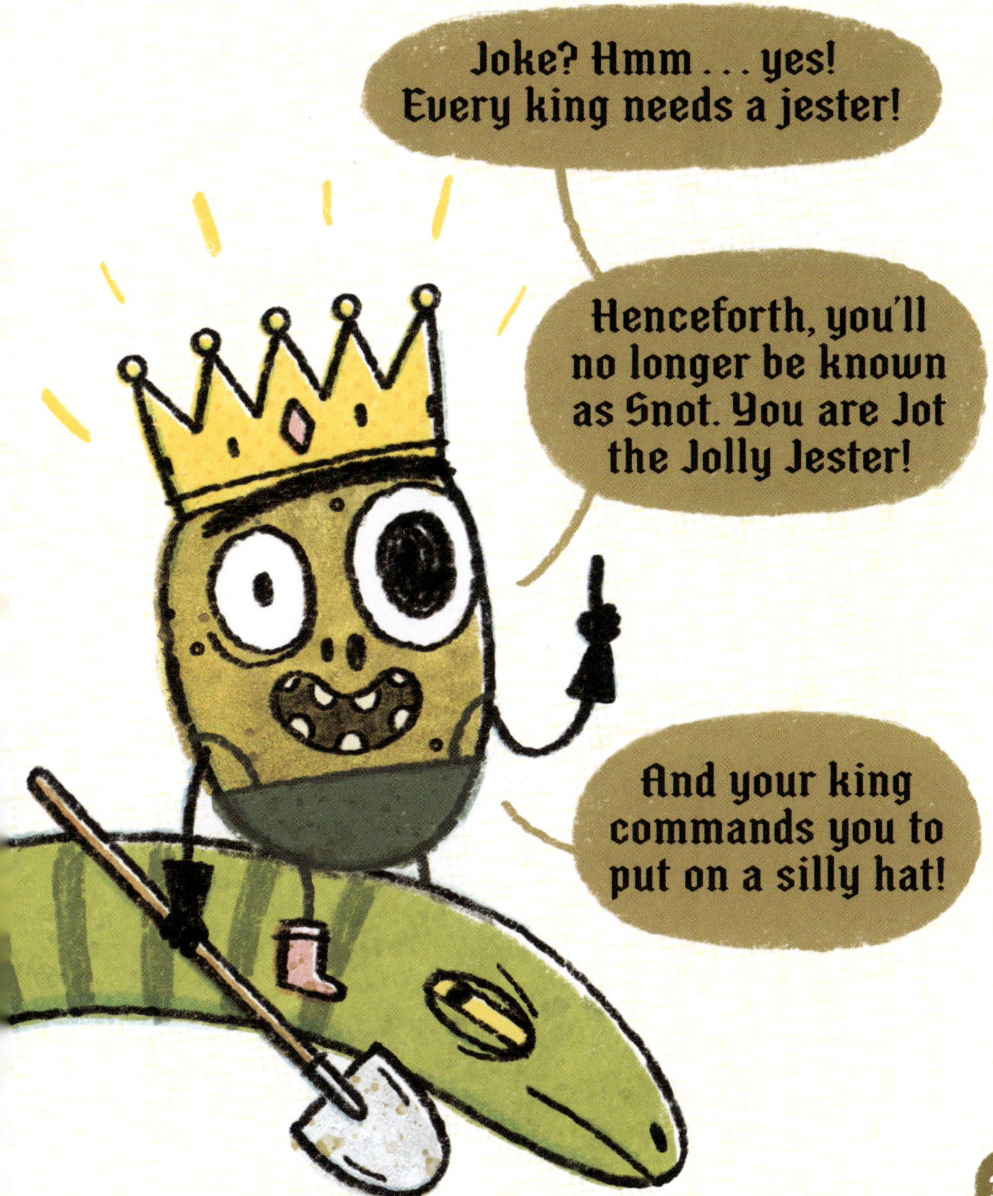
Joke? Hmm . . . yes! Every king needs a jester!
Henceforth, you'll no longer be known as Snot. You are Jot the Jolly Jester!
And your king commands you to put on a silly hat!

And to Snot's disgust he does just that.

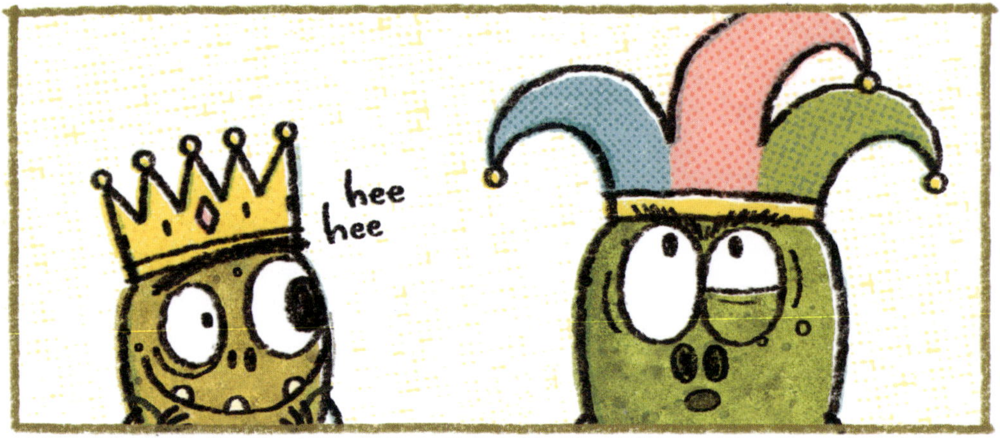
hee
hee

But that is not nearly enough . . . Rot, I mean, His Royal Highness Rotimust Poe Taterust, makes one command after another.

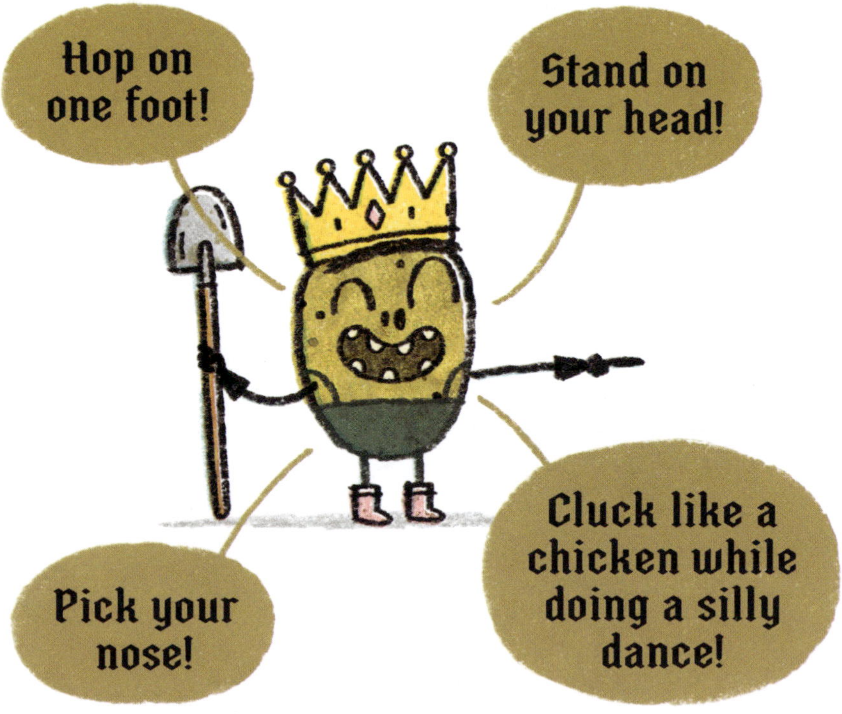
Hop on one foot!
Stand on your head!
Pick your nose!
Cluck like a chicken while doing a silly dance!

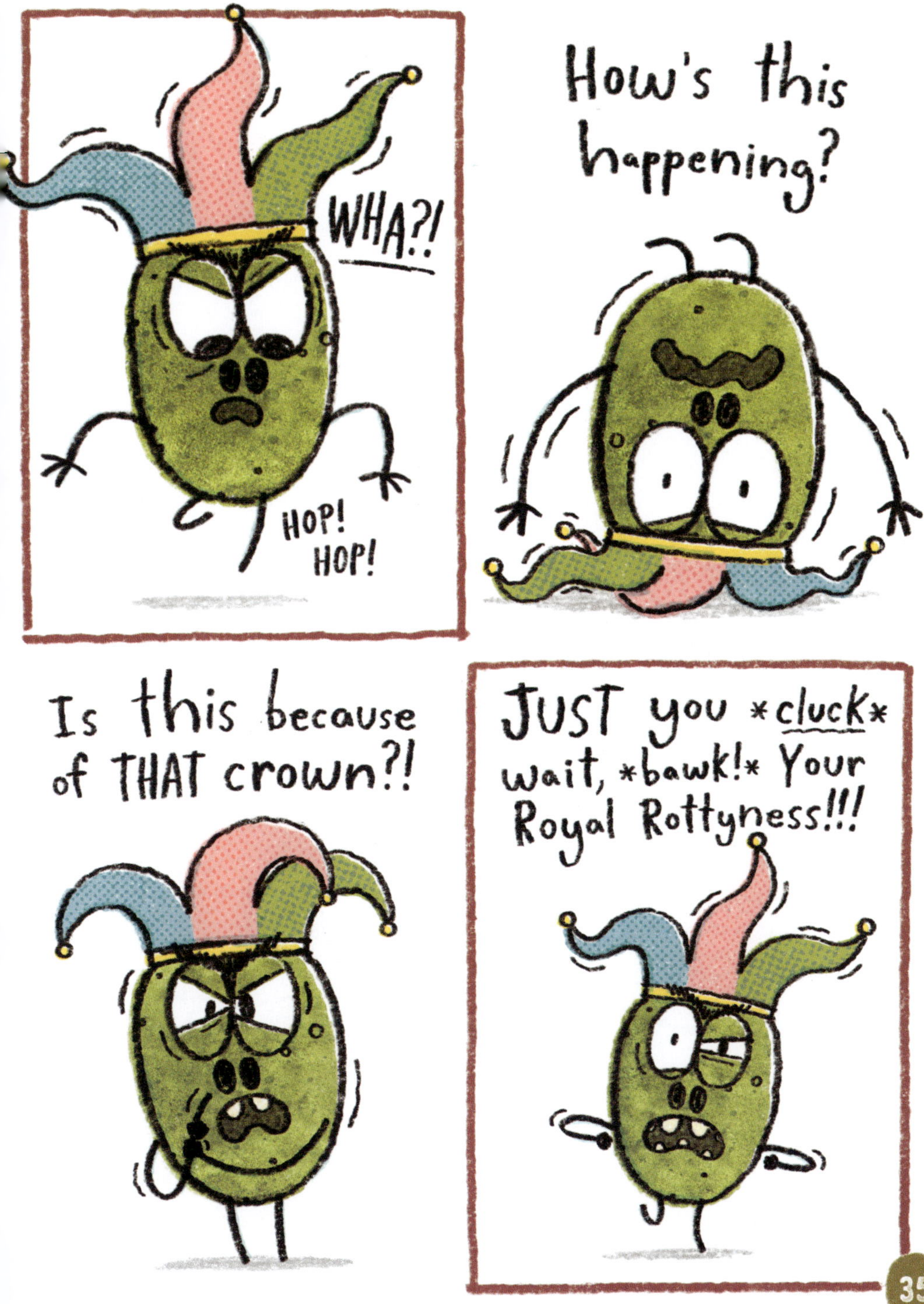
WHA?!
HOP! HOP!
How's this happening?
Is this because of THAT crown?!
JUST you *cluck* wait, *bawk!* Your Royal Rottyness!!!

Snot isn't the only one Rot bosses about.
He commands Tot to fetch him a cape and mirror.

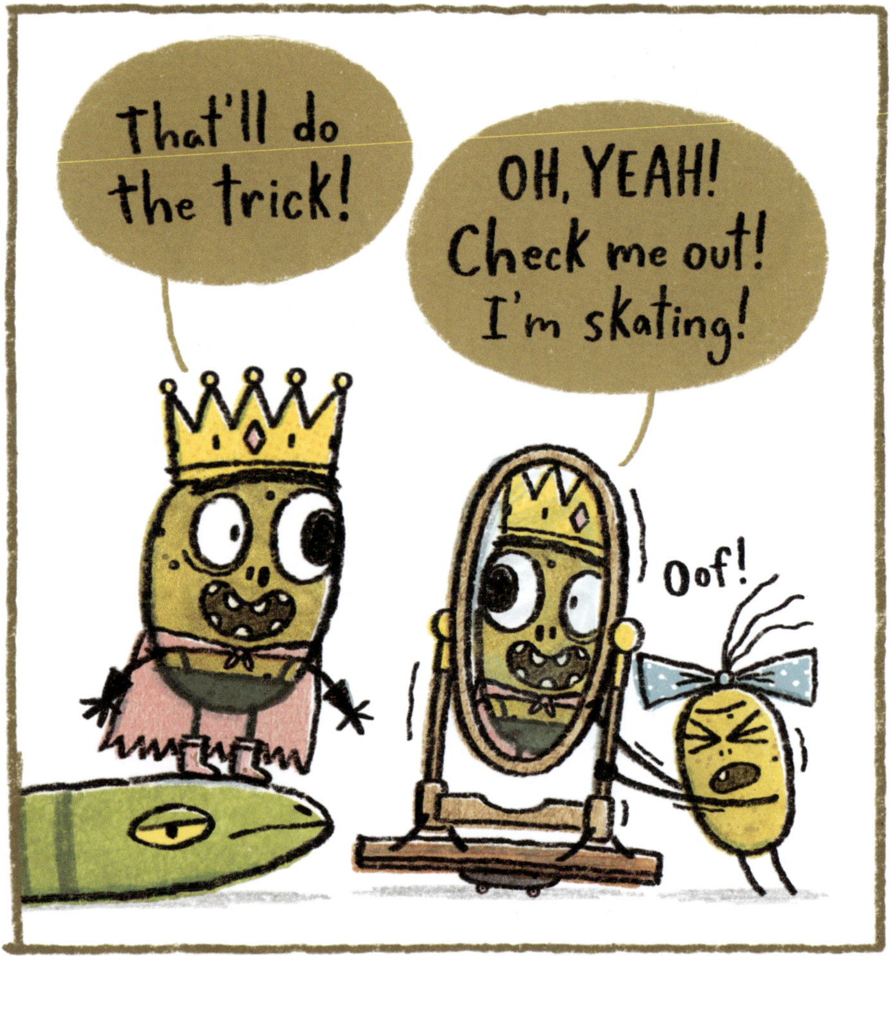
That'll do the trick!
OH, YEAH! Check me out! I'm skating!
Oof!

As for Worm . . .

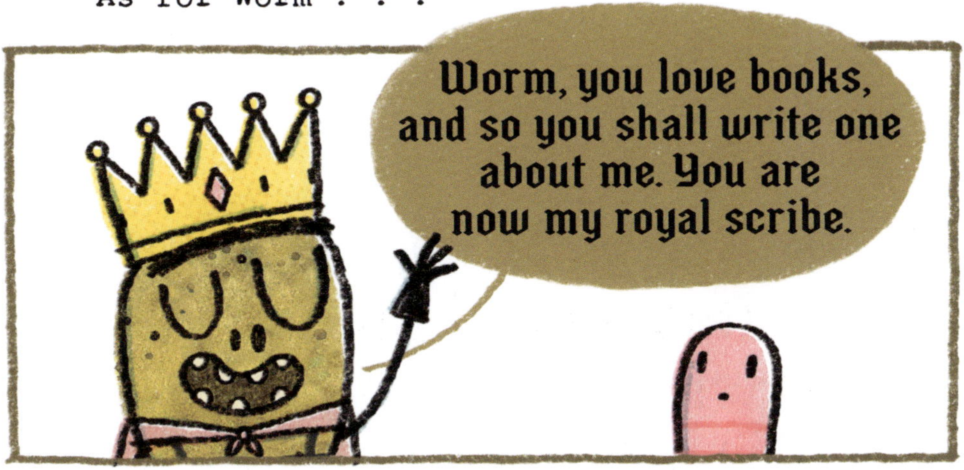
Worm, you love books, and so you shall write one about me. You are now my royal scribe.

Then he orders all his subjects, including a mole and a gnome who had the misfortune of being nearby, to build him a castle out of mud.

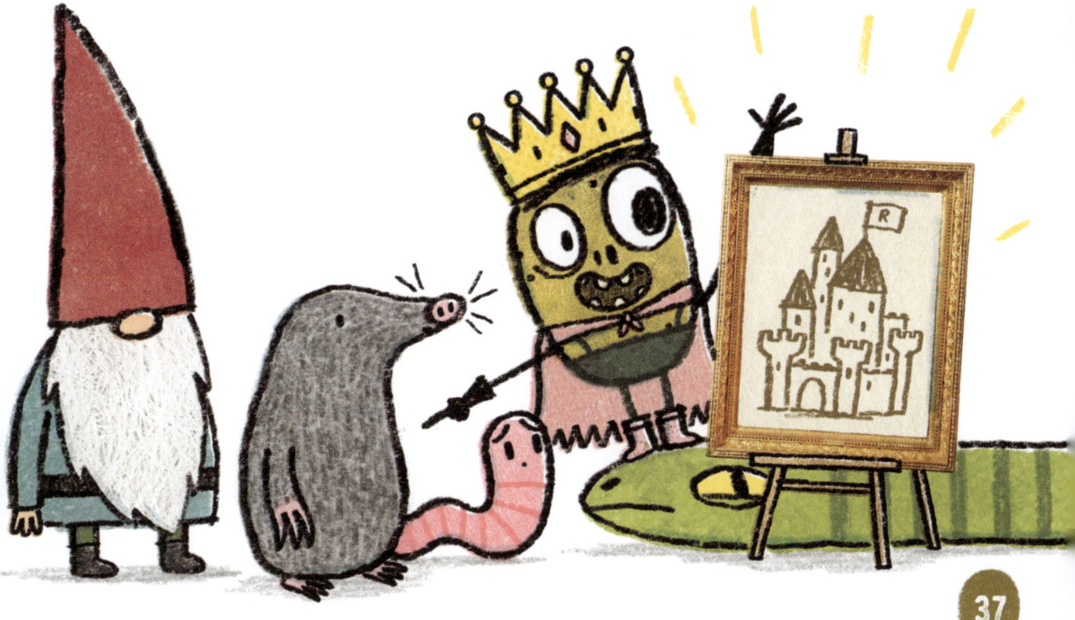
R

And Rot is just getting going. . . .

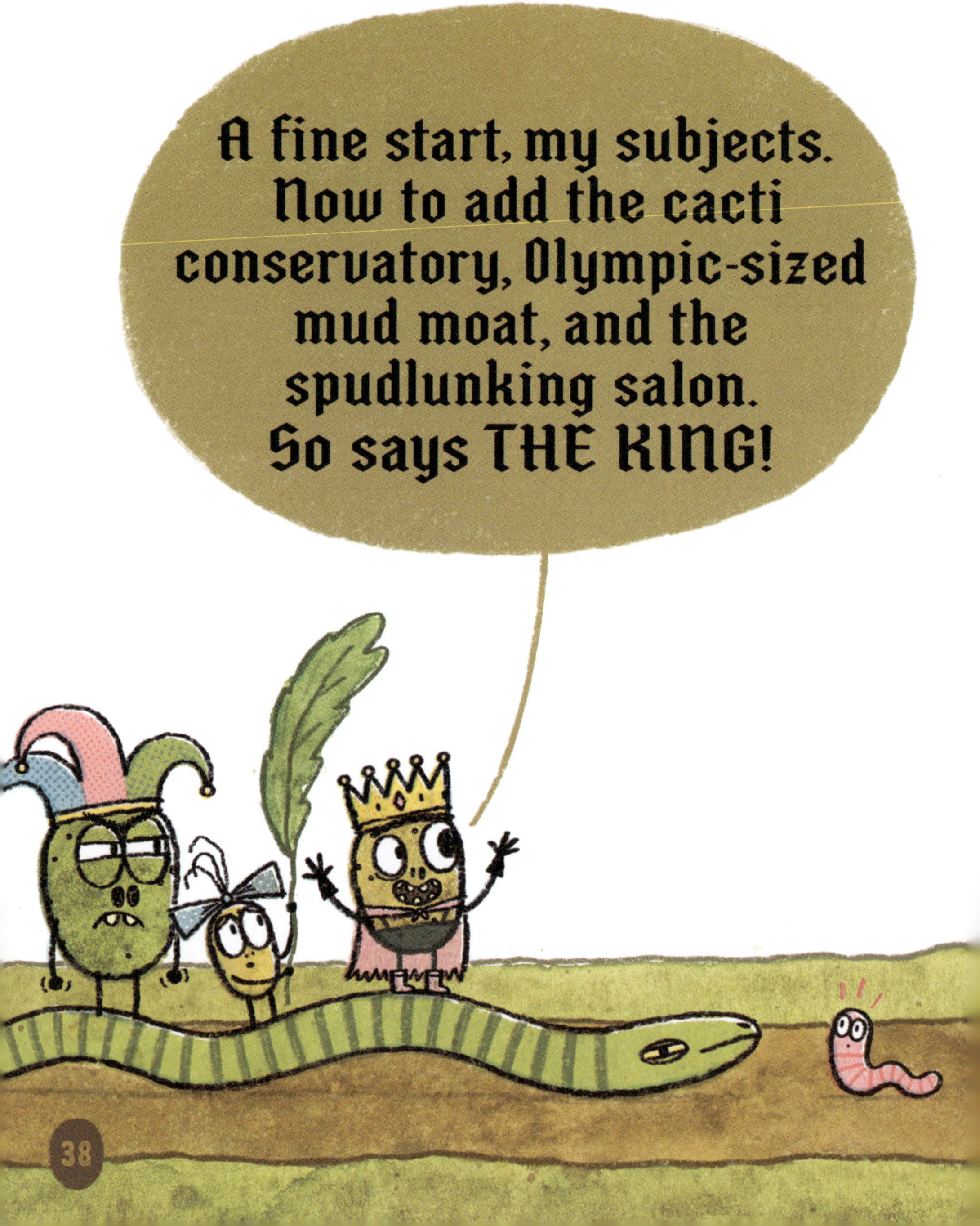
A fine start, my subjects. Now to add the cacti conservatory, Olympic-sized mud moat, and the spudlunking salon. So says THE KING!

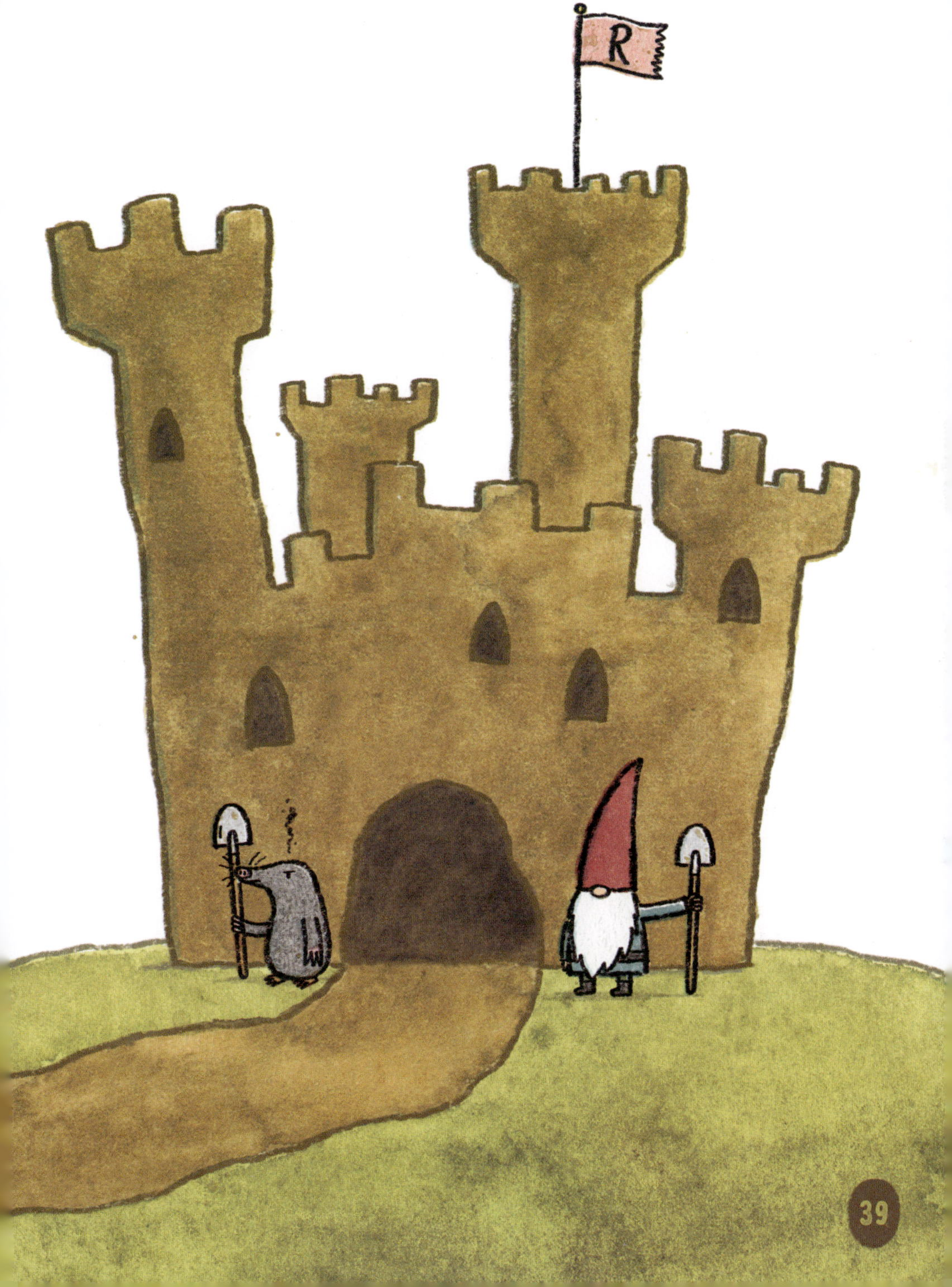
R

CHAPTER 4
DOWN WITH THE KING

With construction of his castle nearly complete, His Royal Highness King Rotimust Poe Taterust heads to the highest tower and commands Tot to bring him a spyglass so he can better view the Realm of Rotimust.

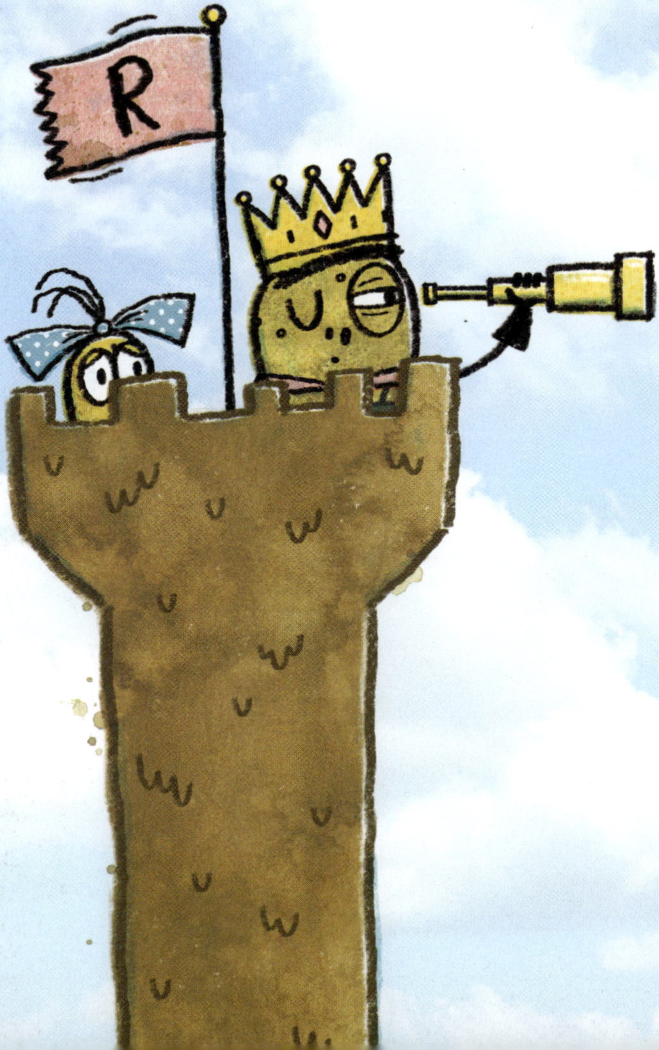
R

He spots some subjects putting the finishing touches on a magnificent mud sculpture.

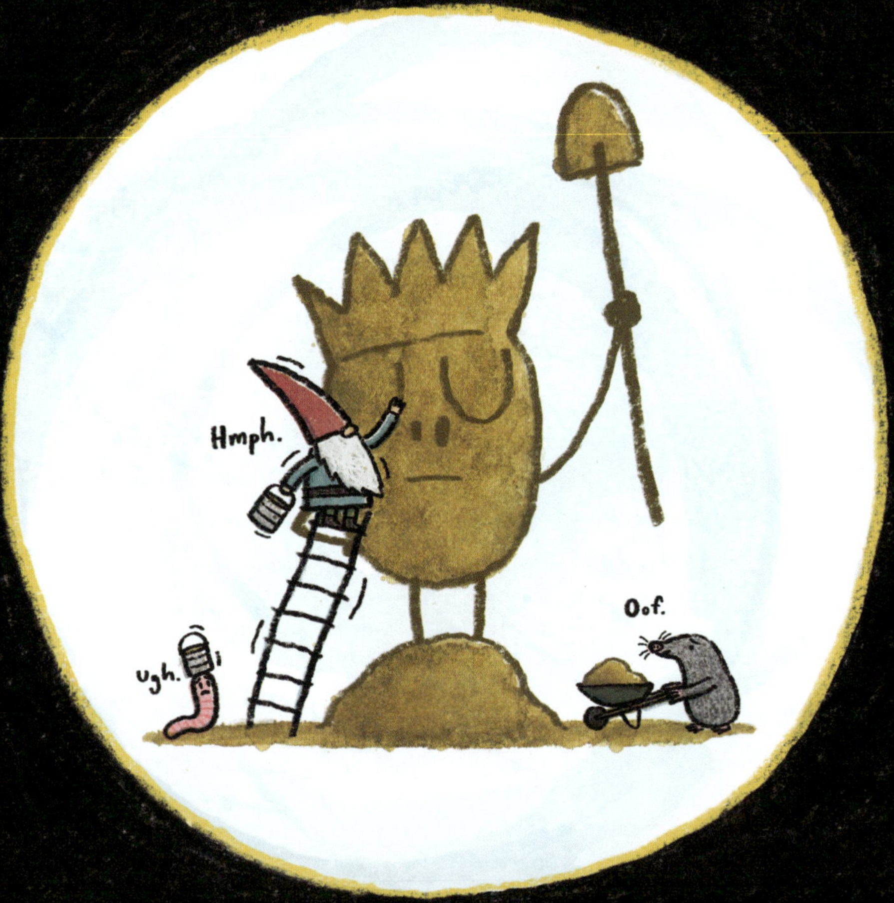
Hmph.
Ugh.
Oof.

He spies Jot the Jolly Jester.

And he sees . . . Tot. His little sister.
She looks . . .

miserable.
Actually, they all do.

Rot doesn't understand. How can anyone be unhappy in such a magnificent kingdom? It has a mud moat and even a cacti conservatory!

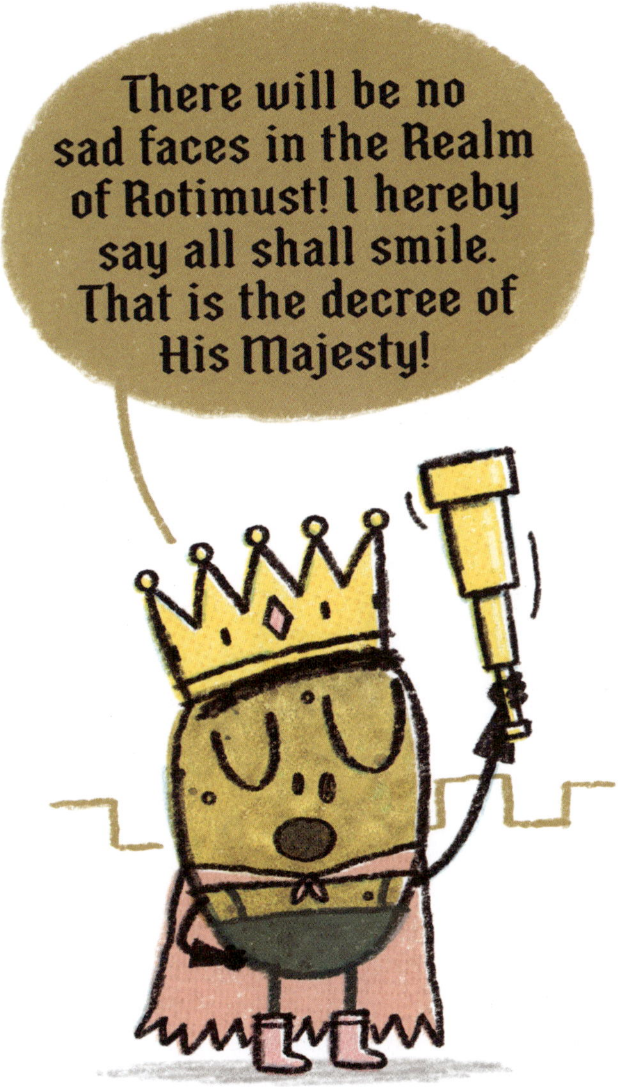
There will be no sad faces in the Realm of Rotimust! I hereby say all shall smile. That is the decree of His Majesty!

Tot smiles, as commanded, or her mouth does at least. But it doesn't reach her eyes.

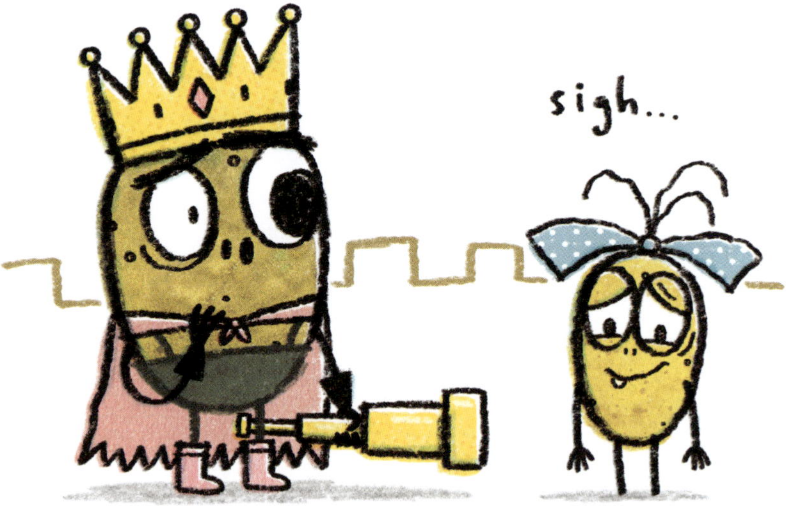
sigh...

Spuddenly (finally!) it occurs to Rot that while he's been having a grand time making everyone do what he wants, maybe it hasn't been very much fun for everyone else.

It is hard to keep having fun when you realize you're the only one.

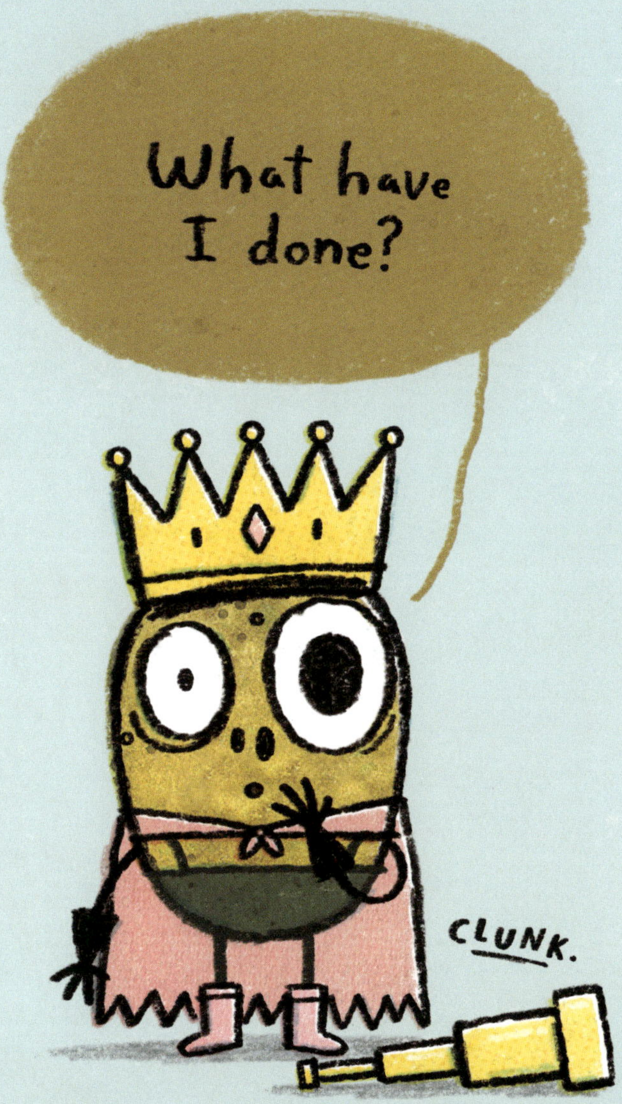
What have I done?
CLUNK.

His Highness King Rotimust Poe Taterust holds court. He gathers all his subjects in the throne room.

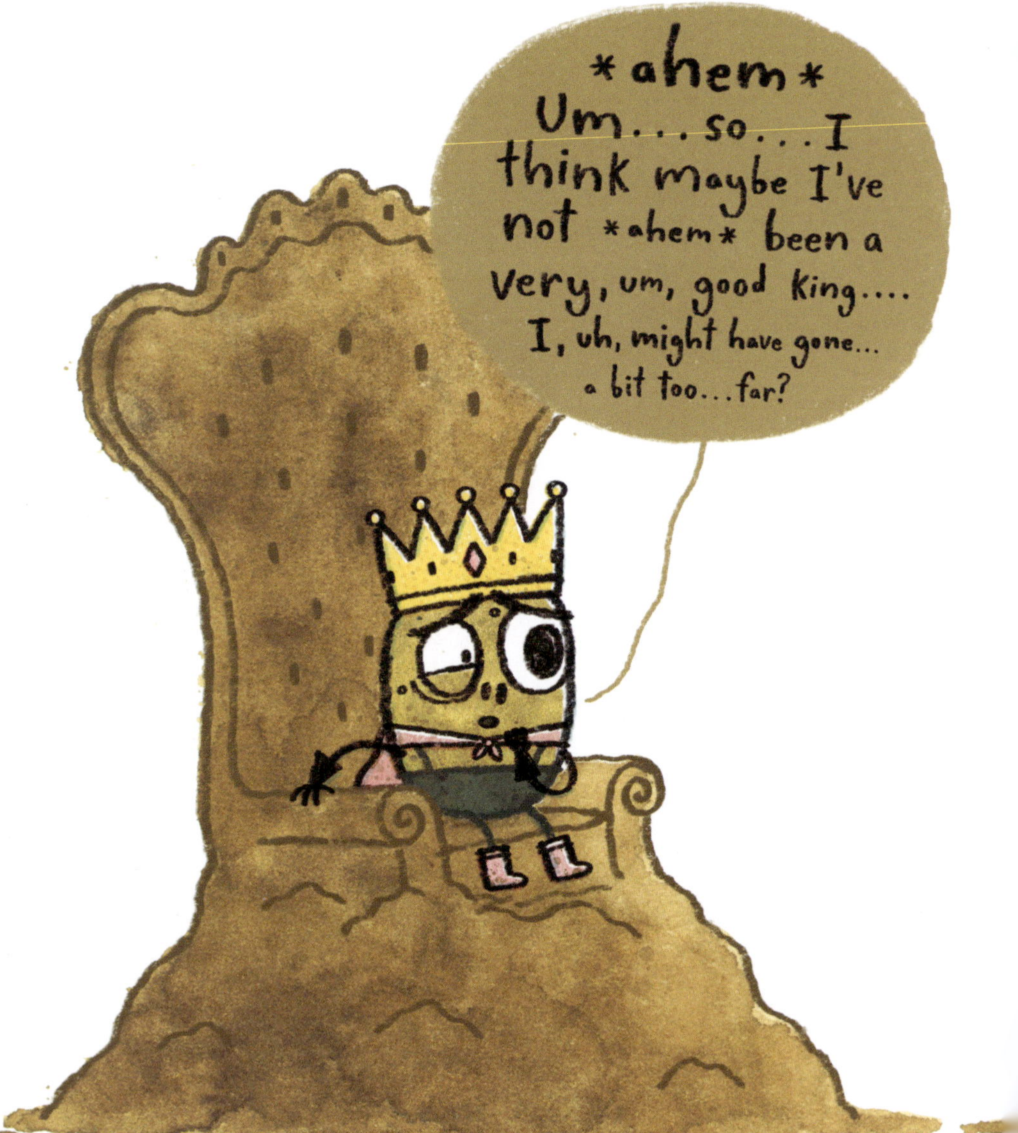
ahem Um... so... I think maybe I've not *ahem* been a very, um, good king.... I, uh, might have gone... a bit too... far?

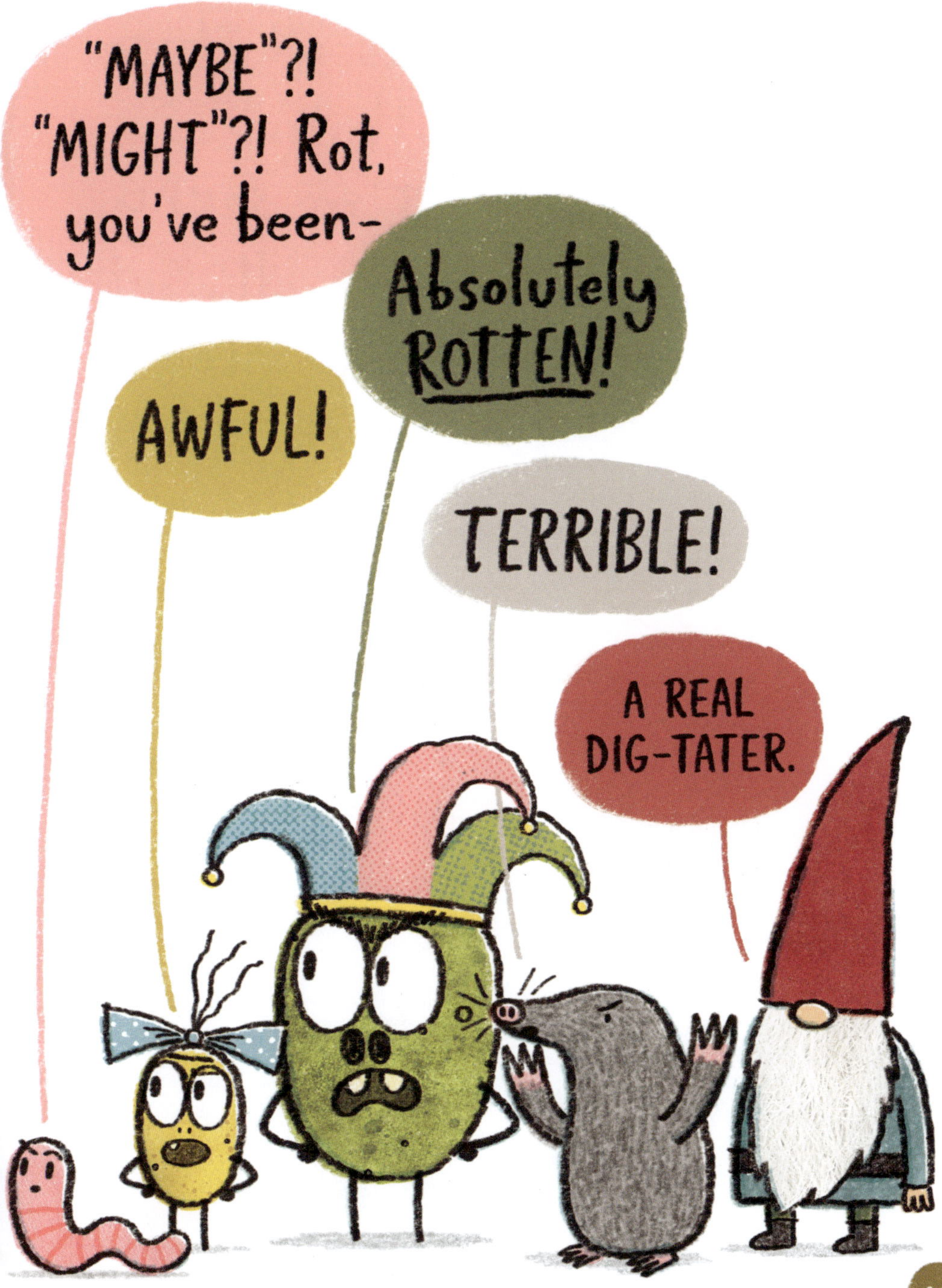
"MAYBE"?! "MIGHT"?! Rot, you've been-
AWFUL!
Absolutely ROTTEN!
TERRIBLE!
A REAL DIG-TATER.

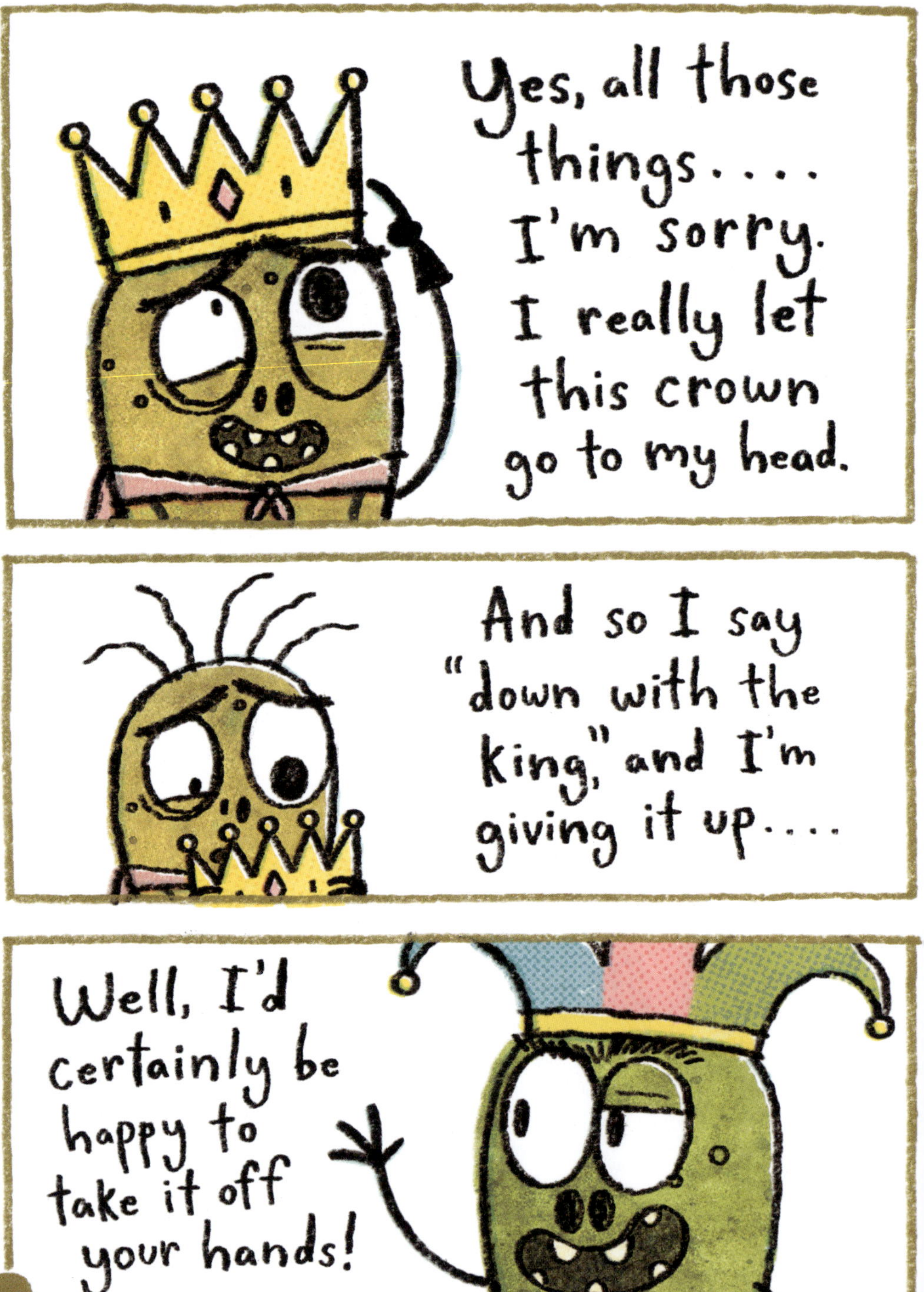
Yes, all those things.... I'm sorry. I really let this crown go to my head.
And so I say "down with the king," and I'm giving it up....
Well, I'd certainly be happy to take it off your hands!

Snot isn't the only one who covets the crown (fancy way of saying they want it really badly).

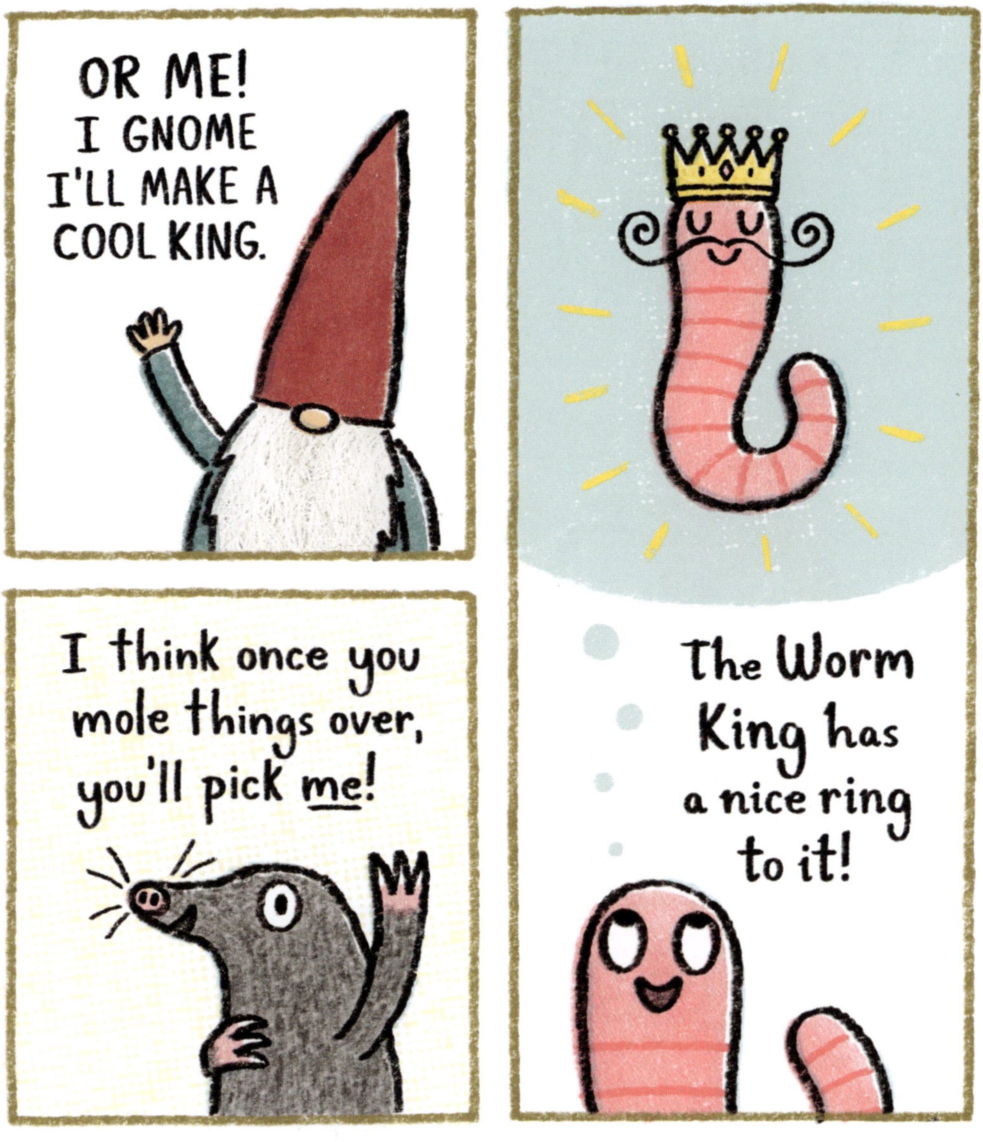
OR ME!
I GNOME I'LL MAKE A COOL KING.
I think once you mole things over, you'll pick me!
The Worm King has a nice ring to it!

Tot is the only one of the lot who doesn't say anything.

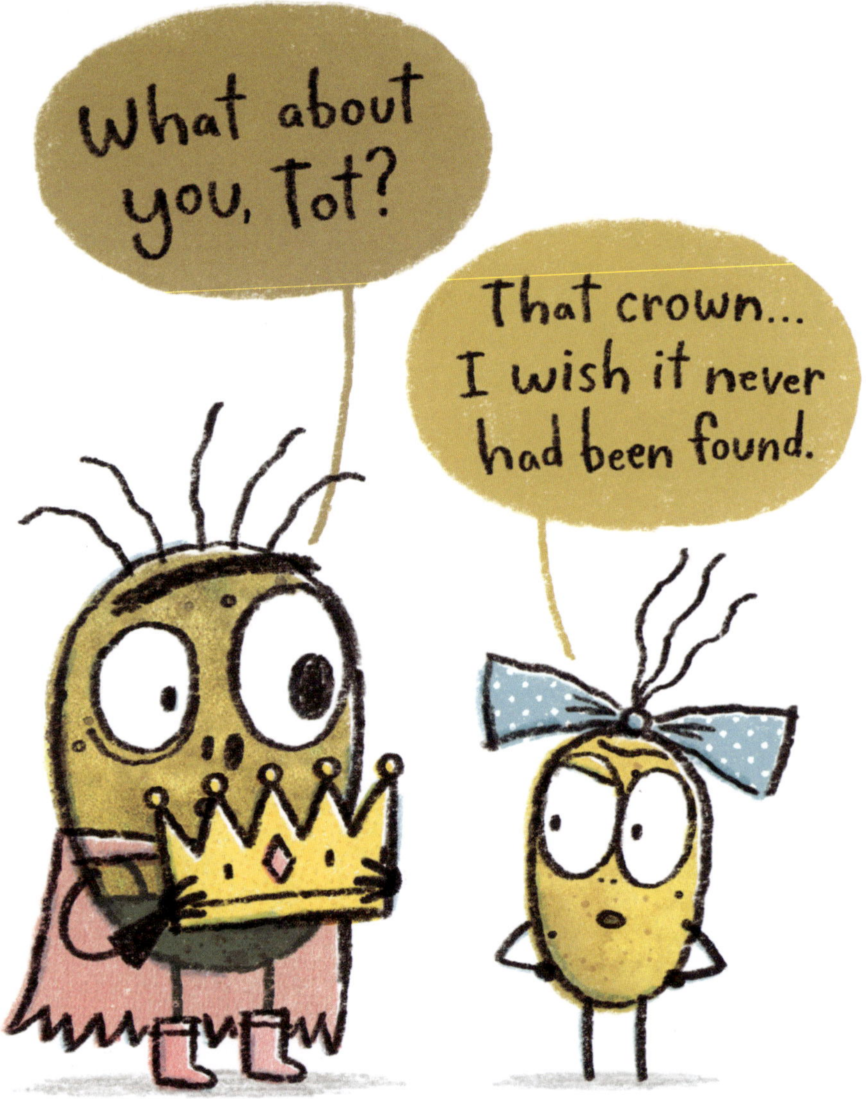
What about you, Tot?
That crown... I wish it never had been found.

This gives Rot a royally great idea.

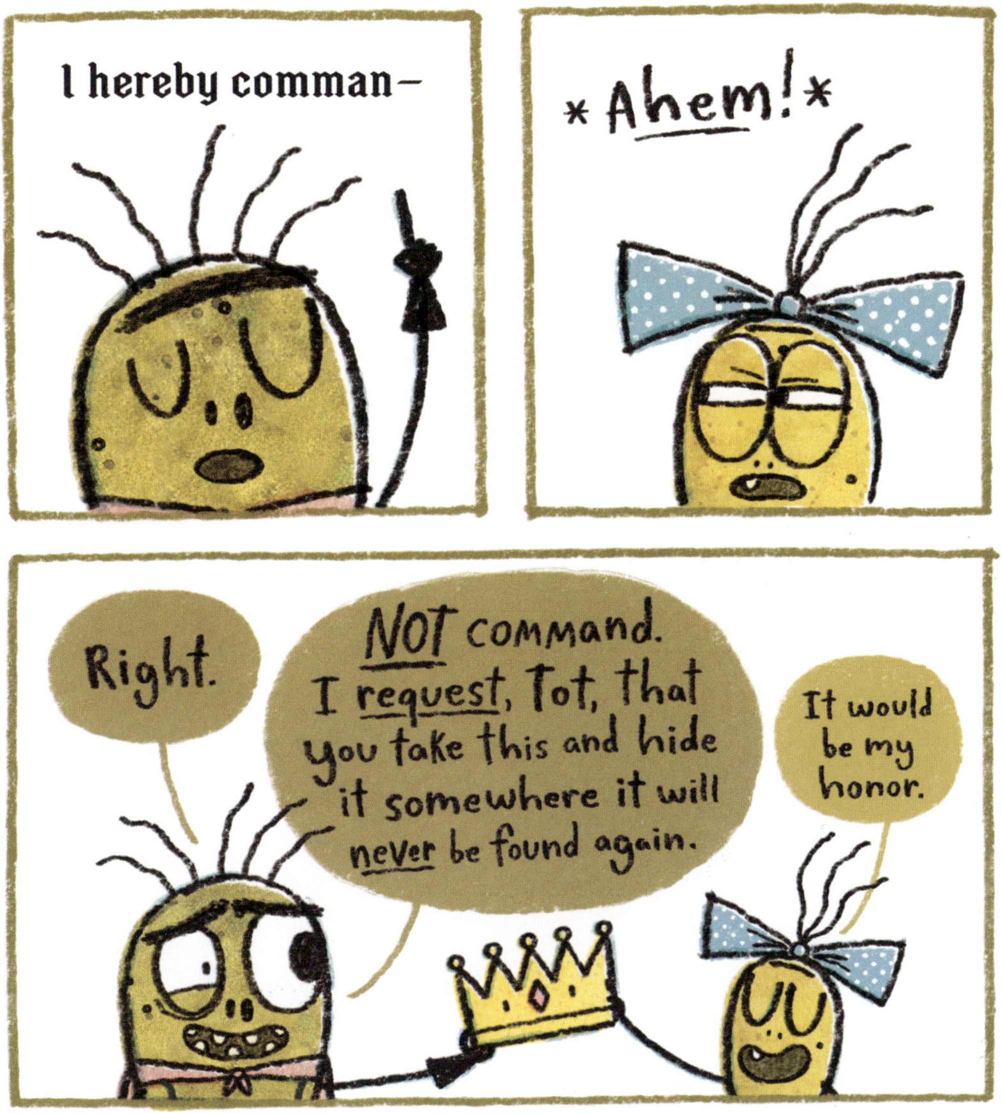
I hereby comman–
Ahem!
Right.
NOT command. I request, Tot, that you take this and hide it somewhere it will never be found again.
It would be my honor.

It takes a minute for him to let go of the crown. But when at last he does, he suddenly feels much lighter. And everyone else (except perhaps Snot) looks happier. This time for real.

CHAPTER 5
THE AMENDs

Apologizing and giving up the crown were a good start, but Rot knows he needs to try to make up for his abysmal (fancy word for "really bad") behavior. He starts by helping Worm with his library.

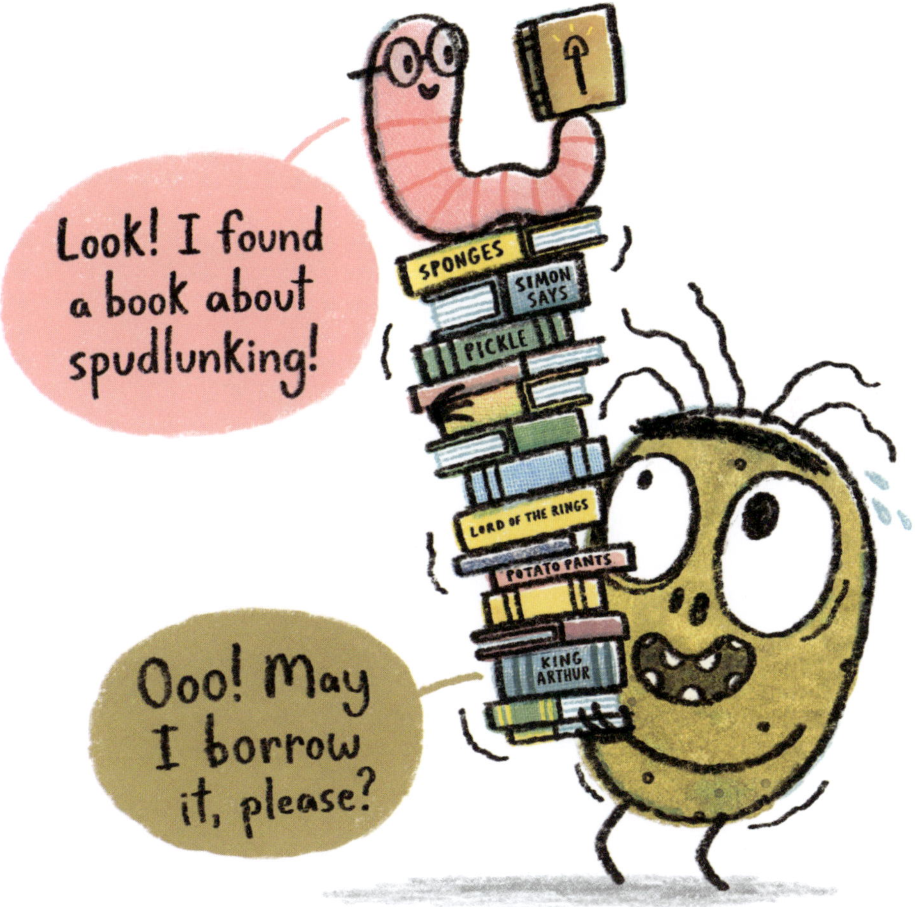
Look! I found a book about spudlunking!
SPONGES
SIMON SAYS
PICKLE
LORD OF THE RINGS
POTATO PANTS
KING ARTHUR
Ooo! May I borrow it, please?

Then Rot helps Tot out with some skateboarding tricks.

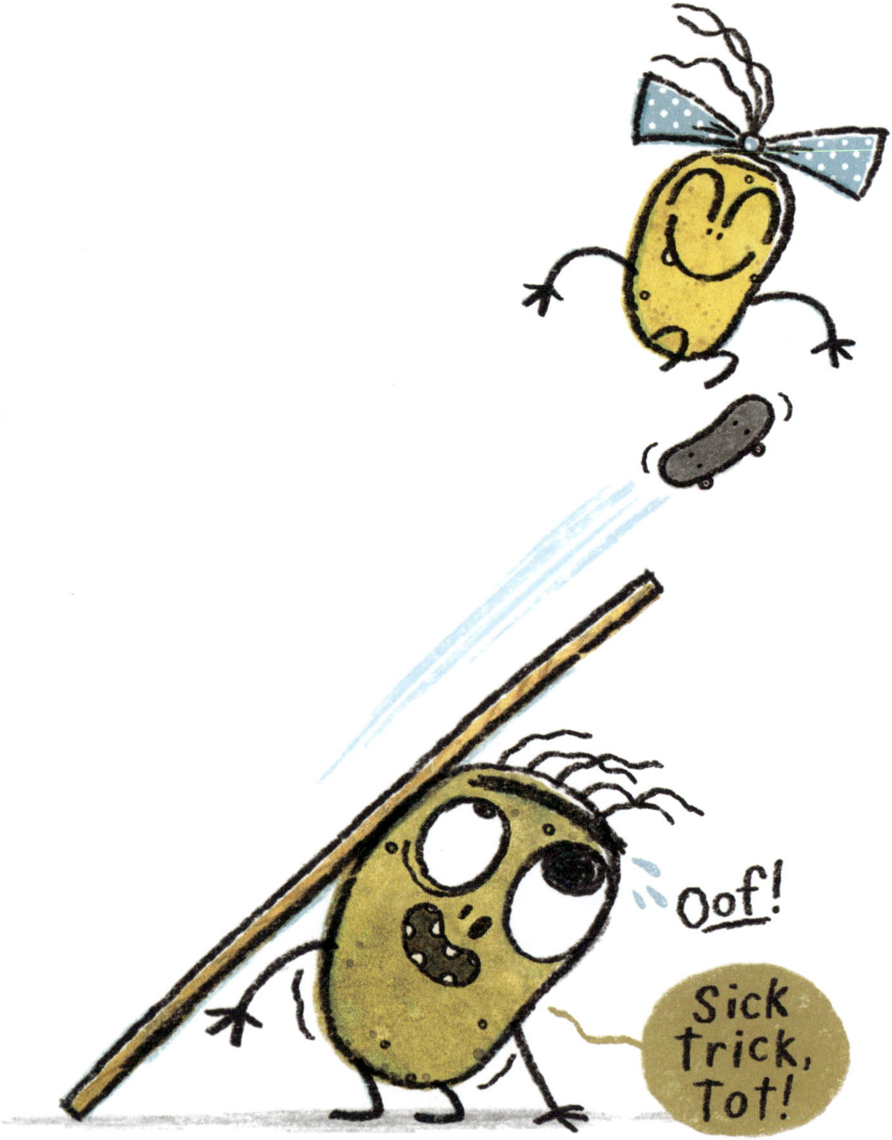
Oof!
Sick trick, Tot!

As for Snot . . .

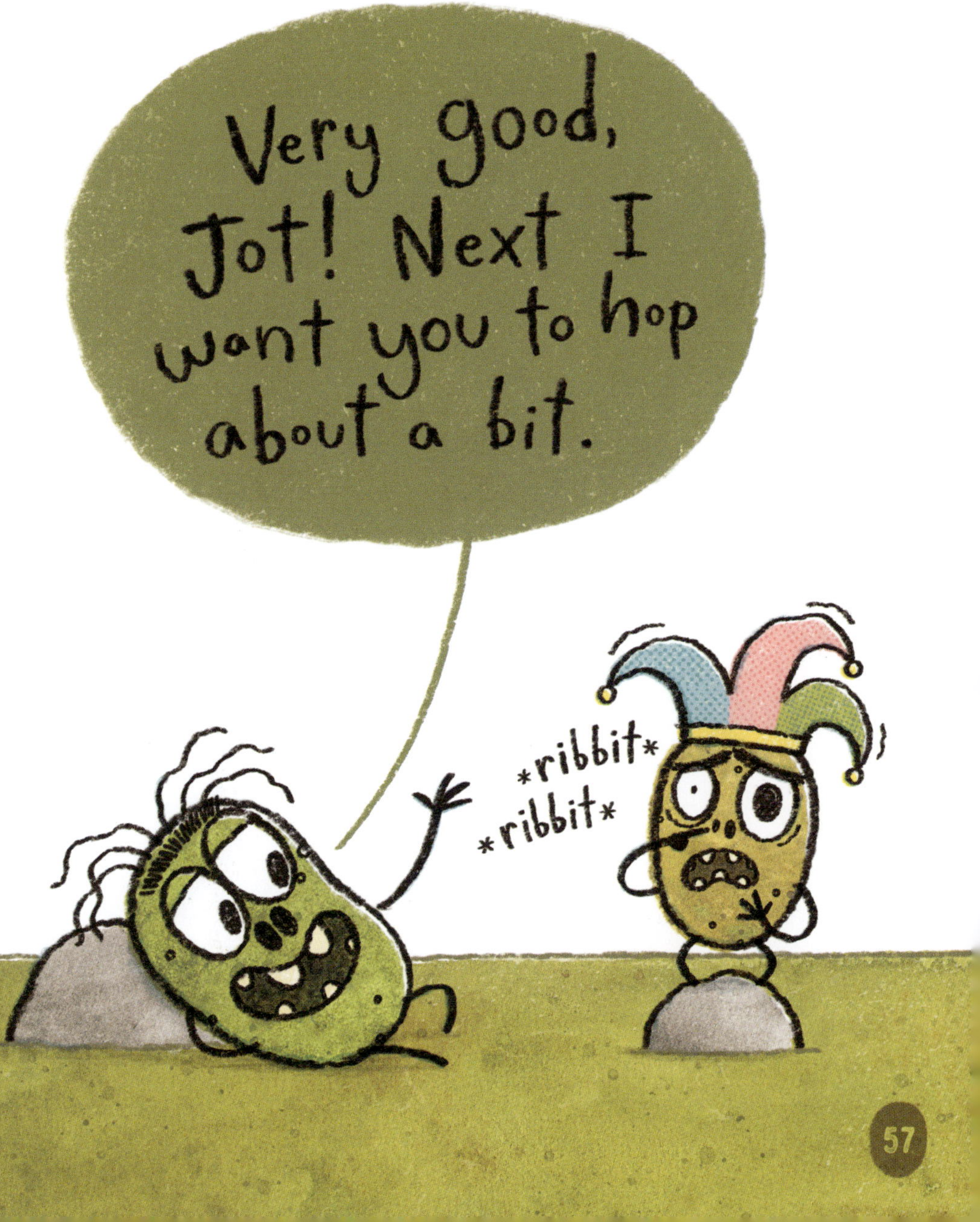
Very good, Jot! Next I want you to hop about a bit.
ribbit
ribbit

Rot wants to make things up to the snake Pretzels, but can't find her anywhere. The first chance she got, she had slithered far far away.

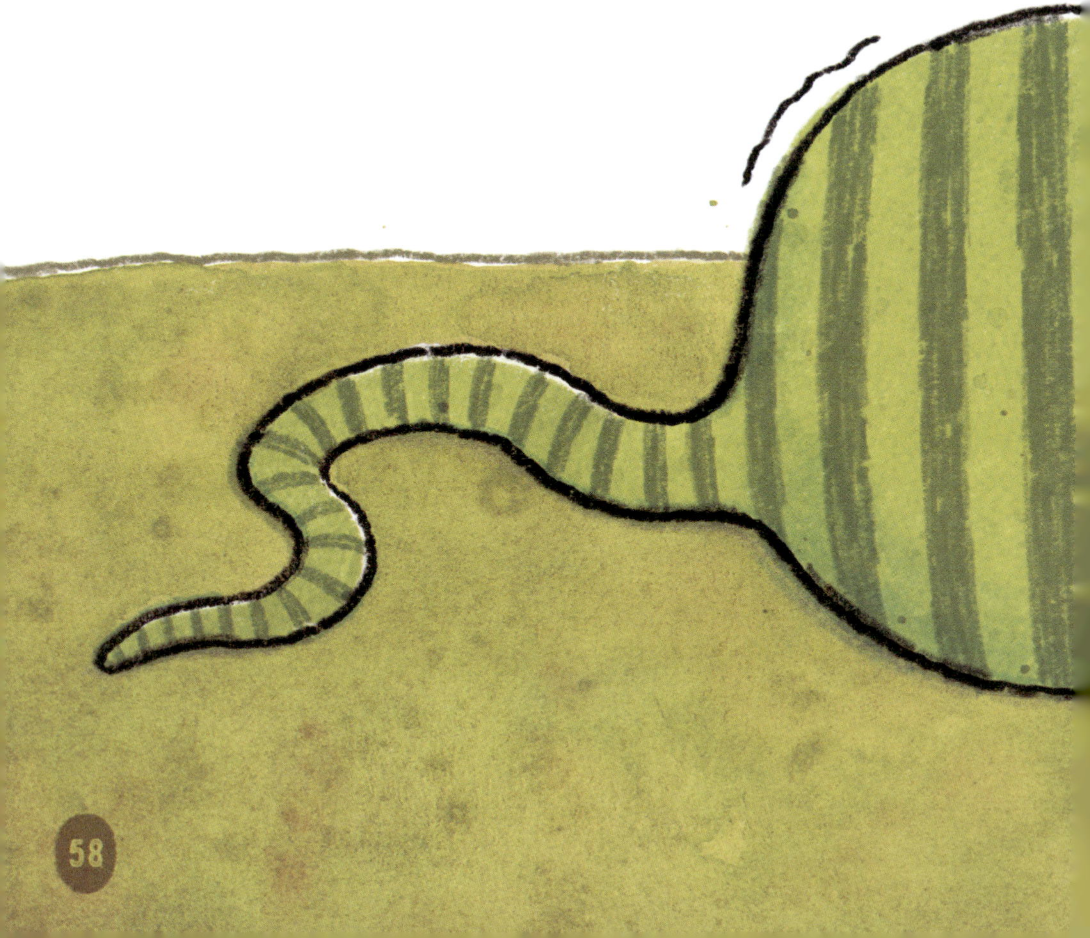

Unfortunately her day doesn't get much better. She mistakes a giant beach ball for an egg, and now has a terrible stomachache.

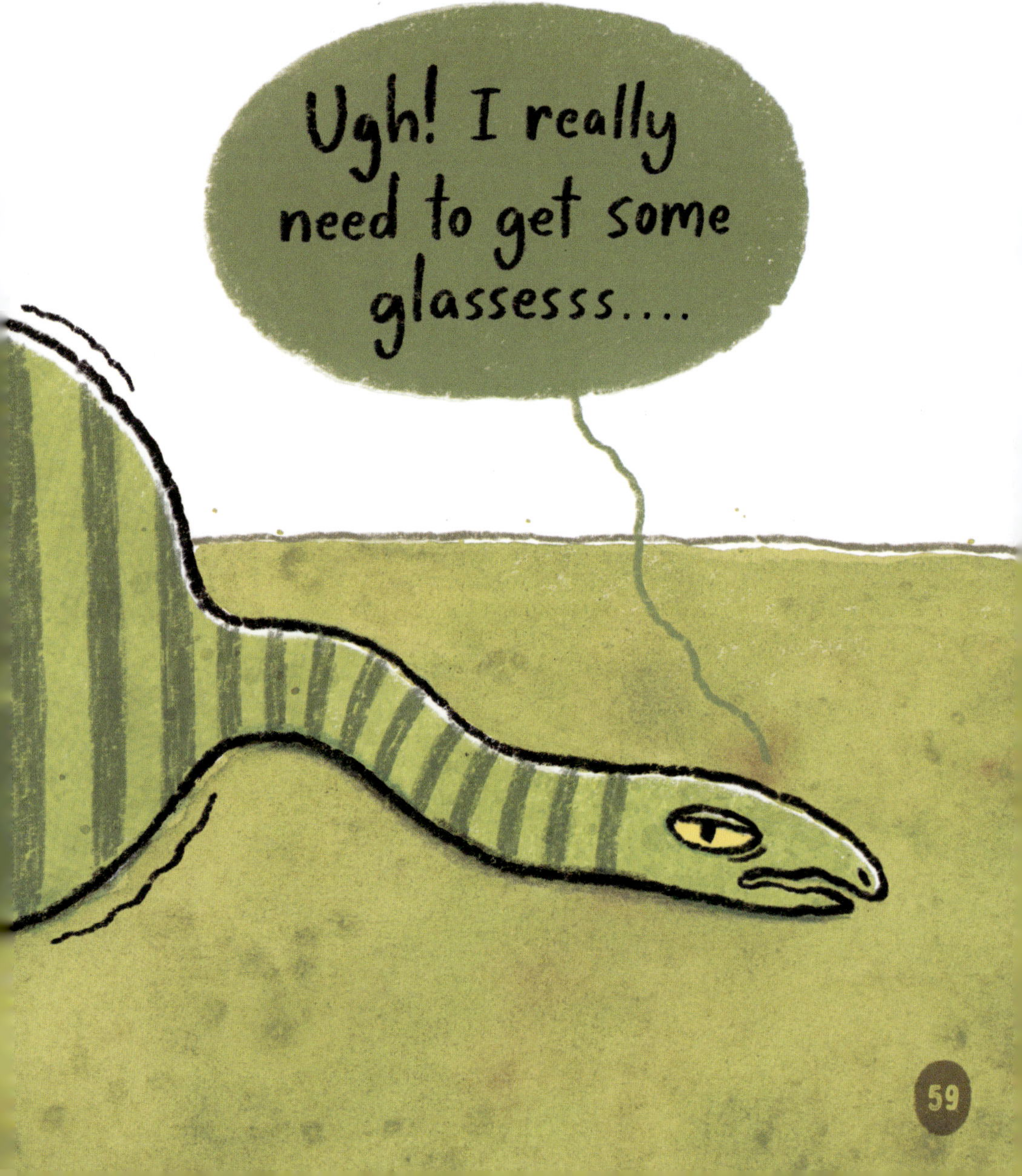
Ugh! I really need to get some glassesss....

Then Rooty the mole has Rot help her with some home renovations she's been meaning to do.

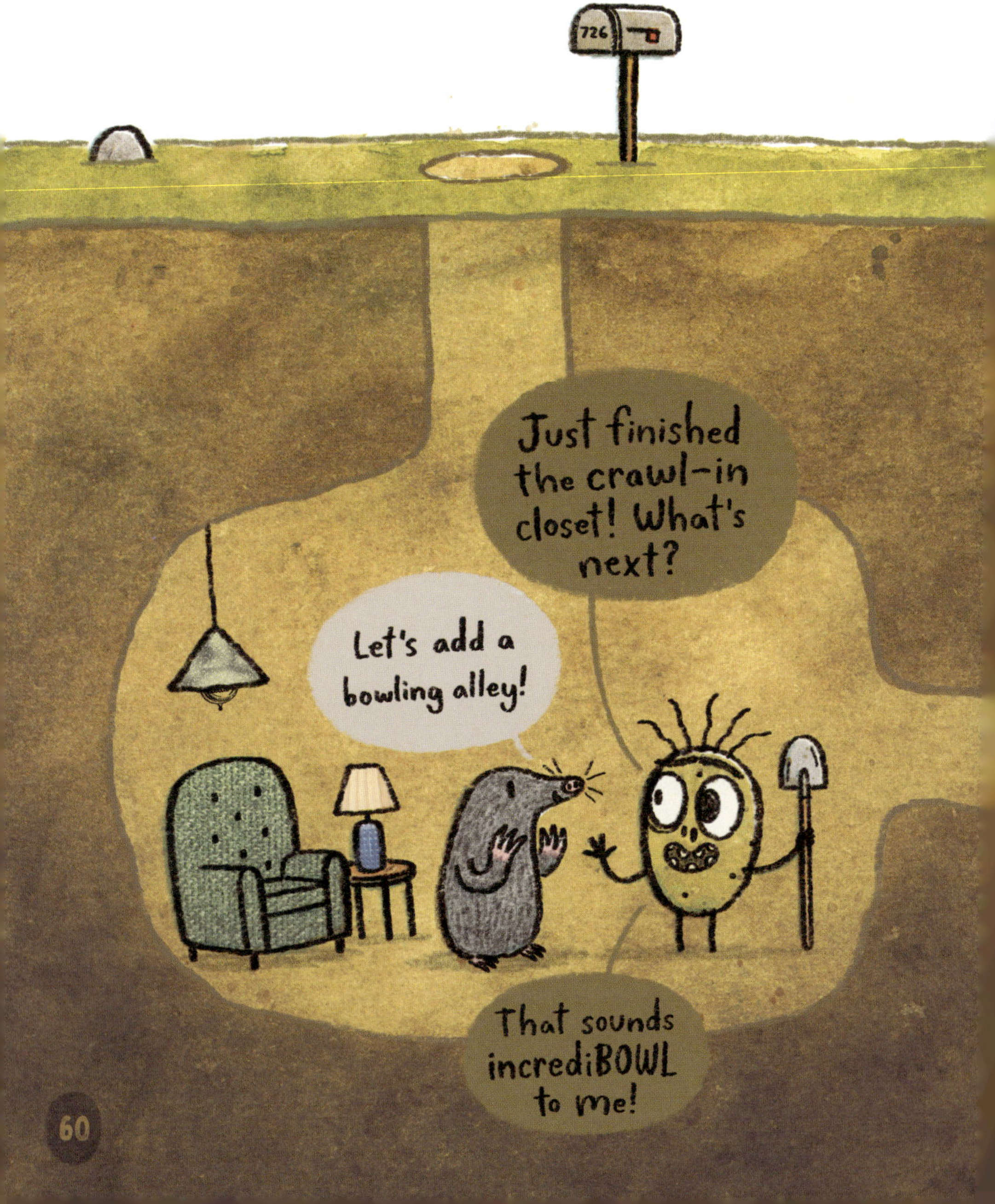
726
Just finished the crawl-in closet! What's next?
Let's add a bowling alley!
That sounds incrediBOWL to me!

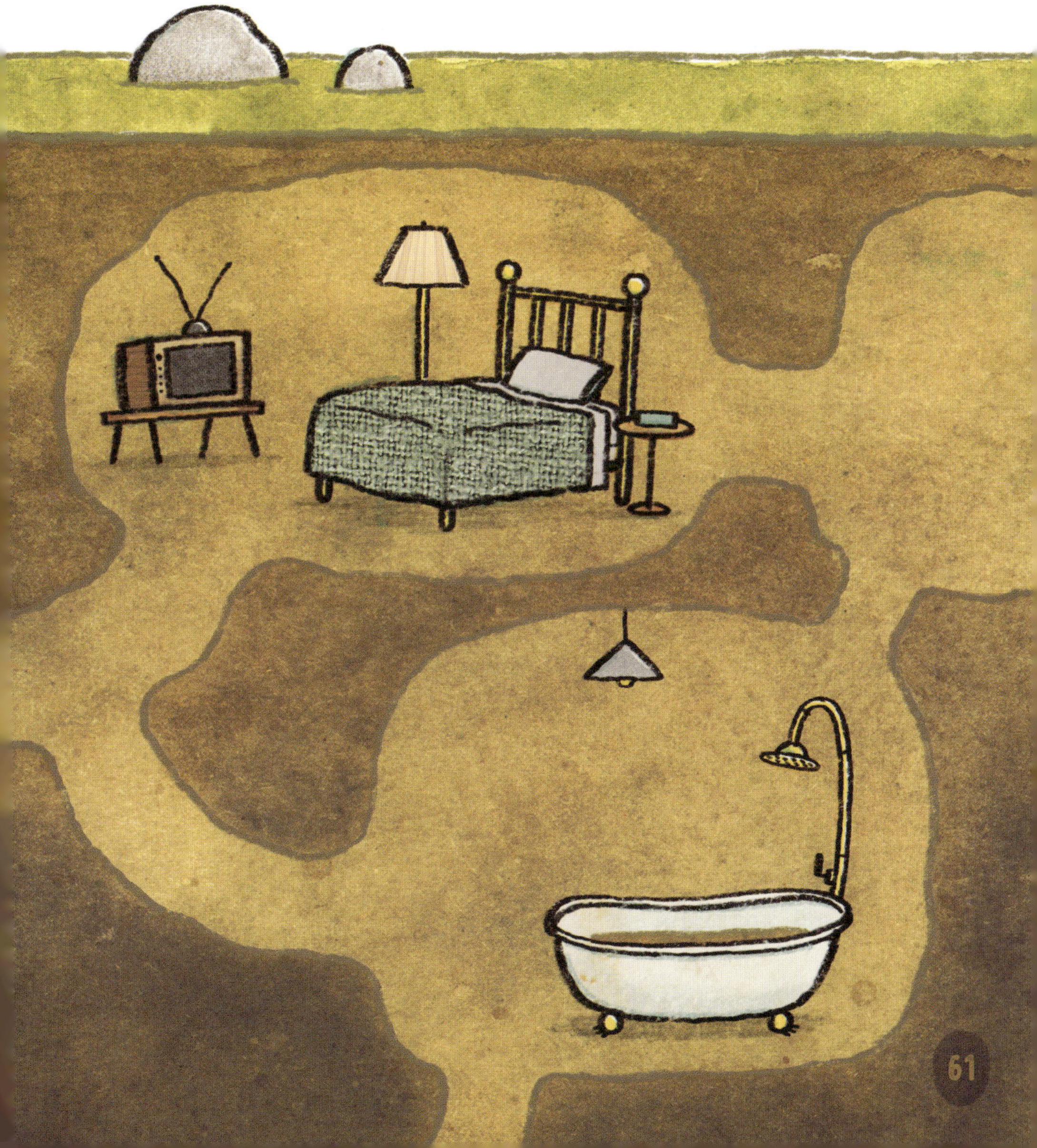

Burgundy the gnome is more than happy to accept one of Rot's spudlunking treasures and call it all even.

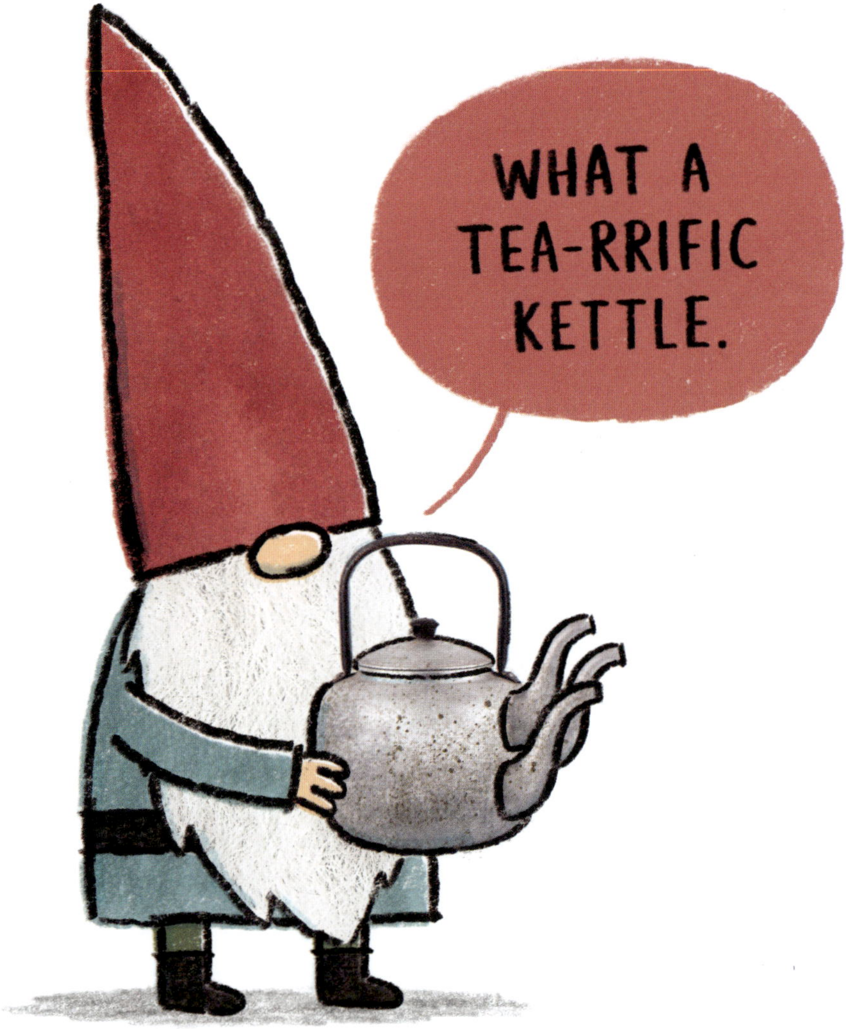
WHAT A TEA-RRIFIC KETTLE.

But will the others ever really forgive Rot? Will they ever want to do something with him again?

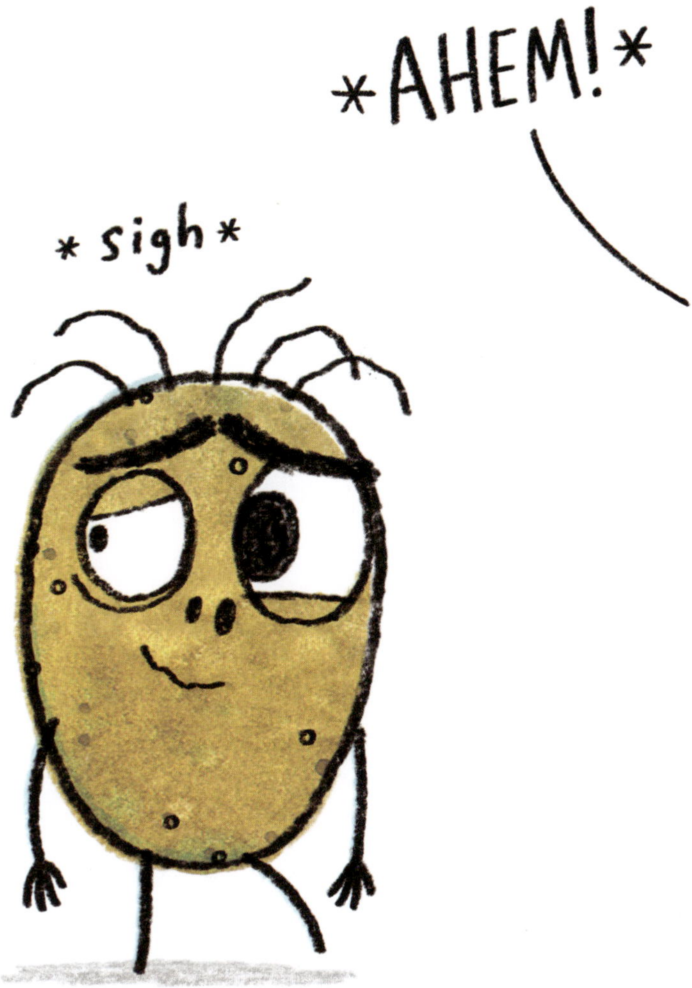
AHEM!
sigh

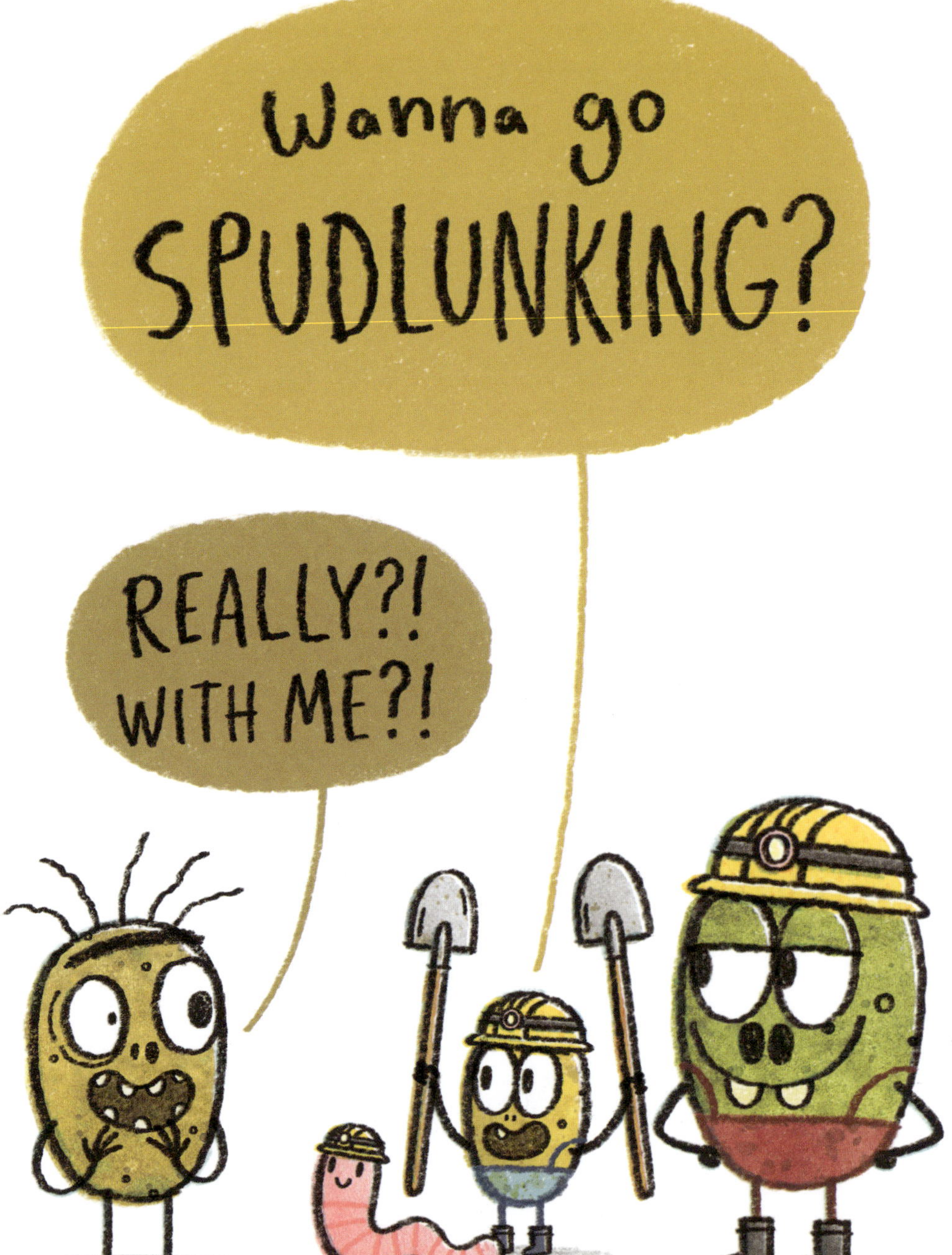
Wanna go SPUDLUNKING?
REALLY?! WITH ME?!

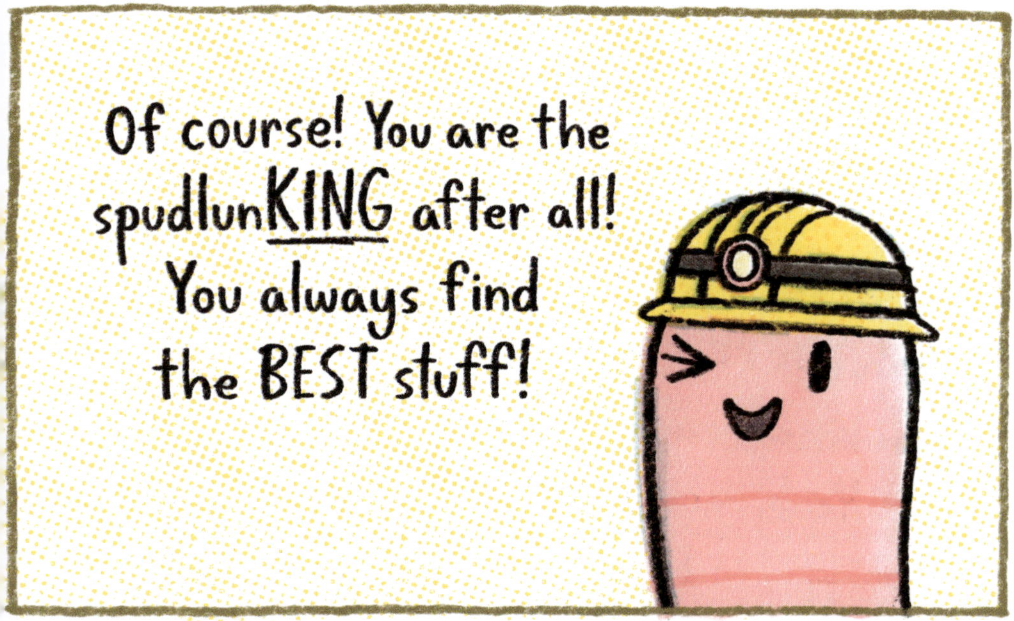
Of course! You are the spudlunKING after all! You always find the BEST stuff!

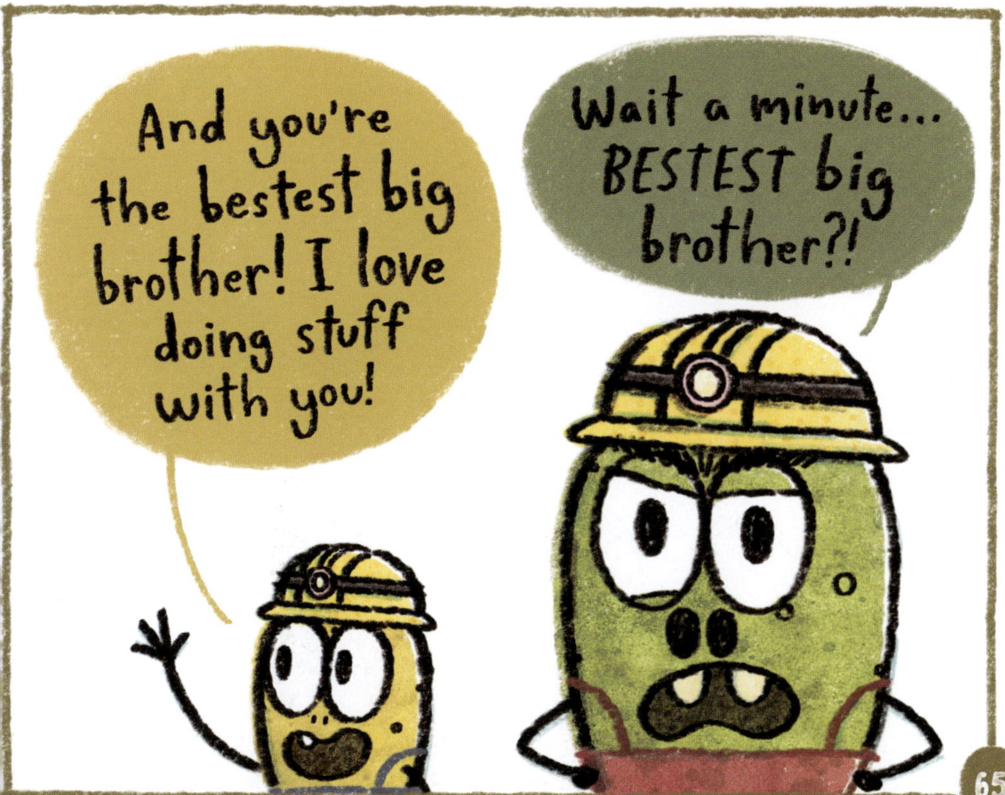
And you're the bestest big brother! I love doing stuff with you!
Wait a minute... BESTEST big brother?!

The spudlunking expedition is a hole bunch of fun!

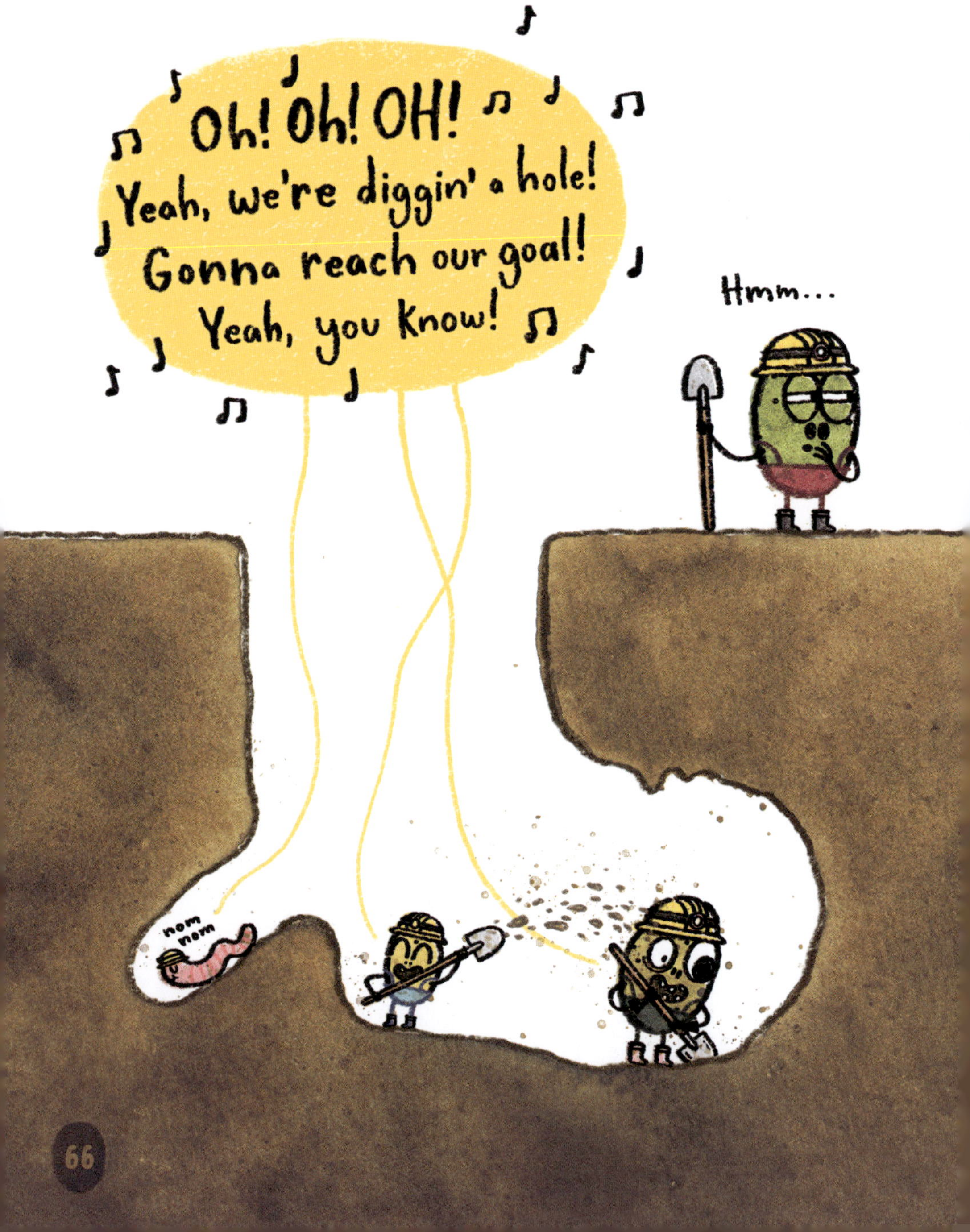

Oh! Oh! OH!
Yeah, we're diggin' a hole!
Gonna reach our goal!
Yeah, you know!
Hmm...
nom nom

Worm unearths a whole box of books!

What a treasure!

Tot is digging the unicycle she found.

This thing is wheely fun!

And Rot found a pot!

Doris? That's a GREAT name for a cactus!
DORIS

But what has become of Snot?

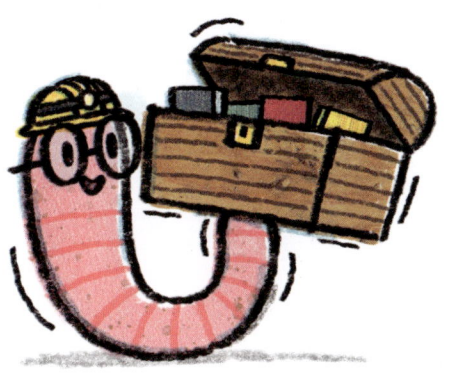

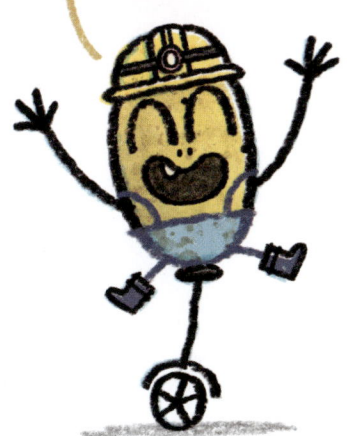

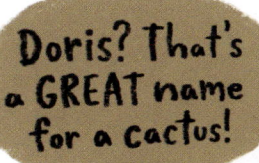

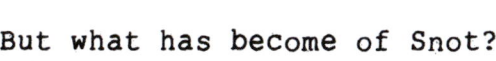

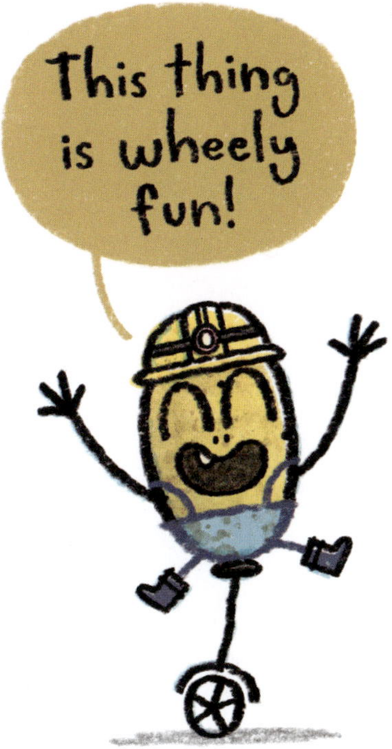

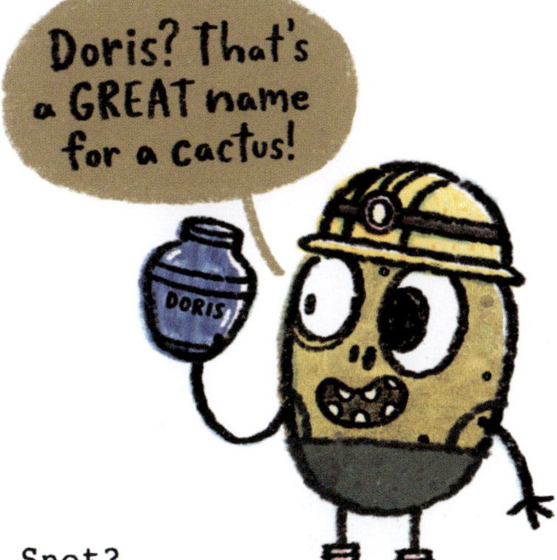

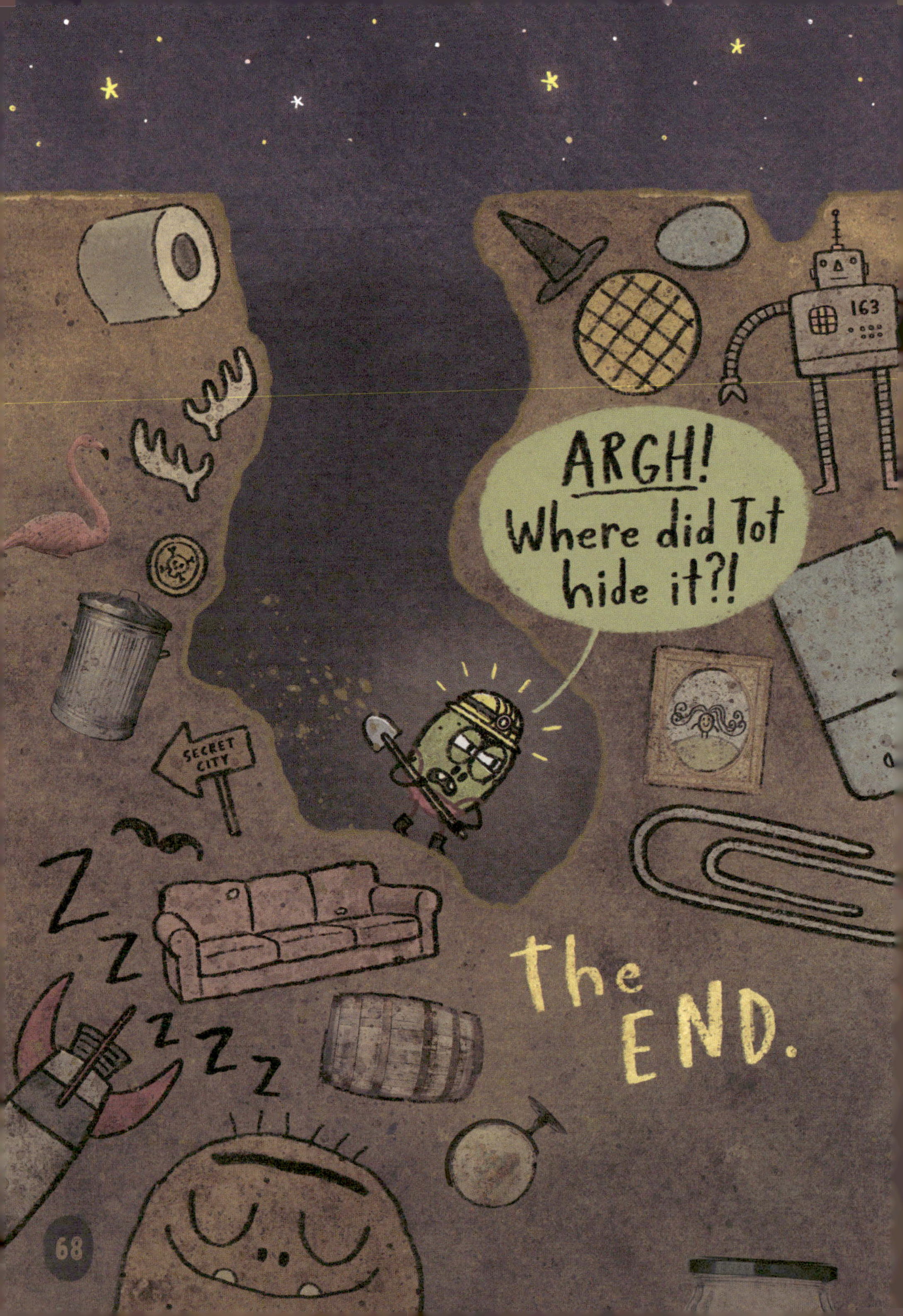

ARGH! Where did Tot hide it?!
163
SECRET CITY
Z Z Z
Z Z Z
the END.

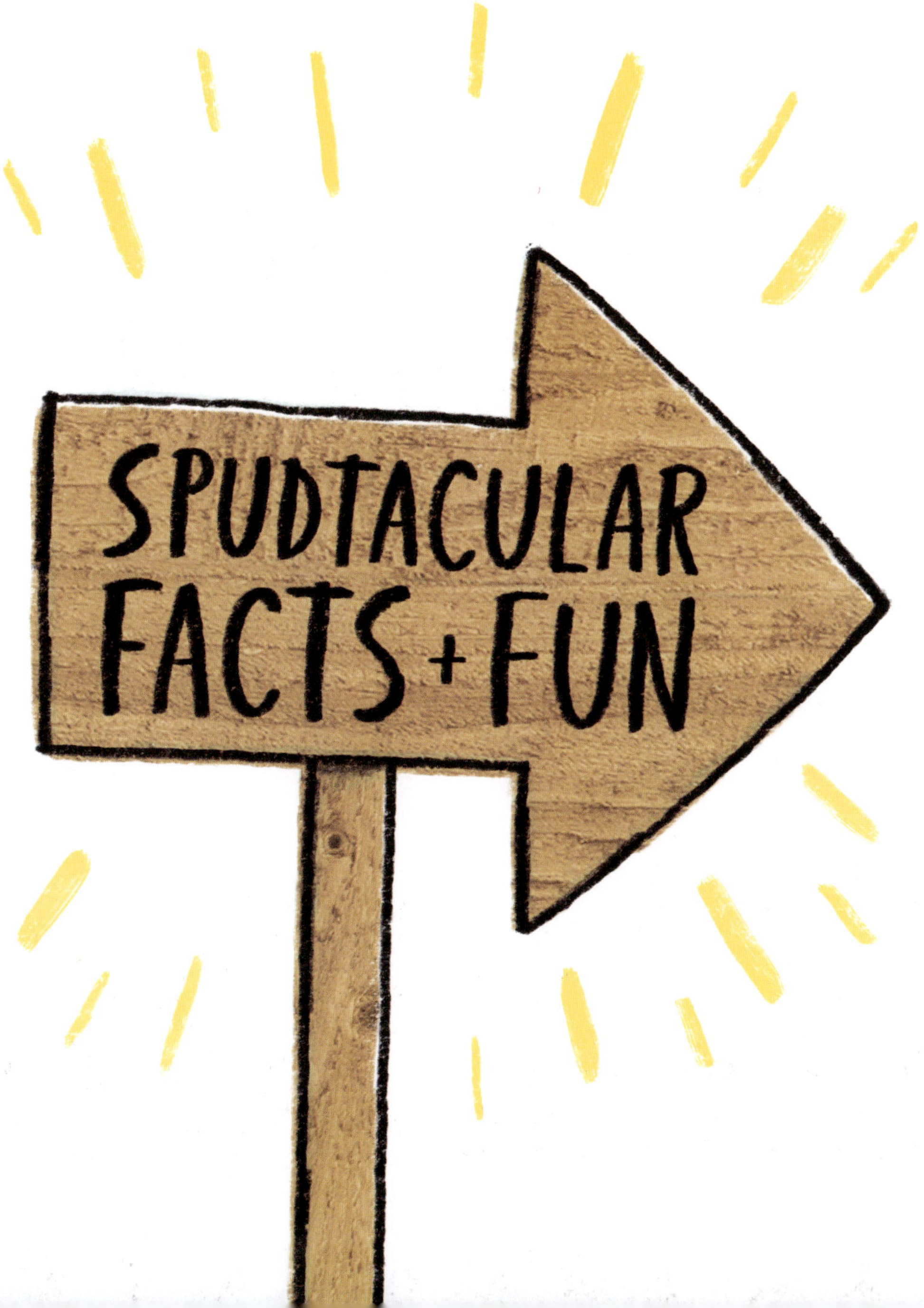
SPUDTACULAR
FACTS + FUN

SPUDTACULAR FACTS

REAL STUFF PEOPLE HAVE DUG UP!

In 1978 a couple of kids discovered a Ferrari buried in a yard in Los Angeles.

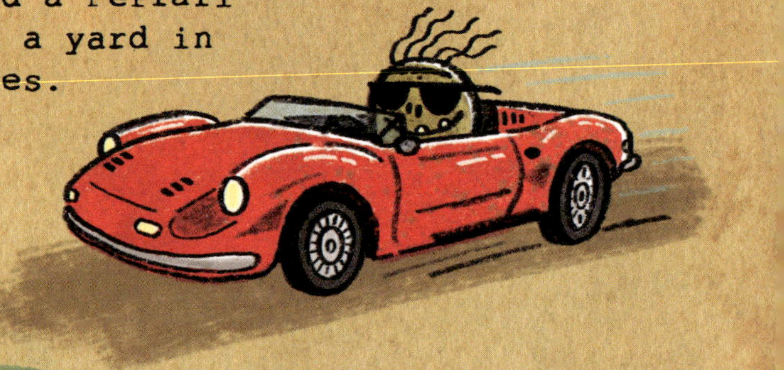

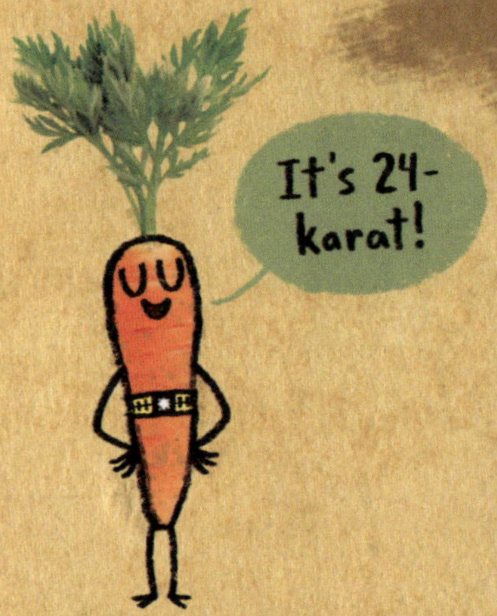
It's 24-karat!

A diamond ring that had been lost for thirteen years was found around a carrot in a vegetable patch.

A 13,000-year-old mastodon skeleton was unearthed in Hyde Park, New York, during a pond renovation.

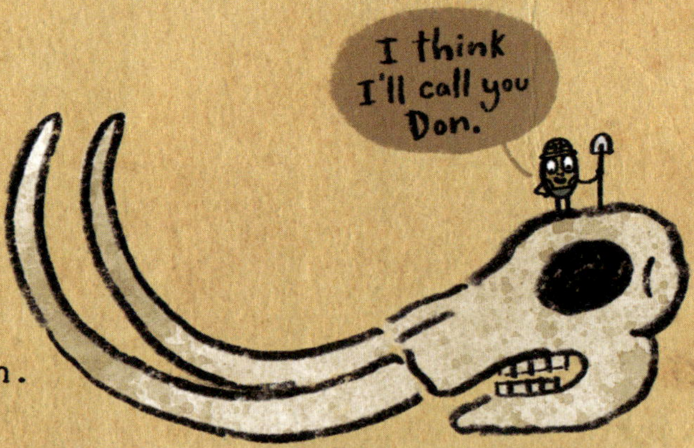
I think I'll call you Don.

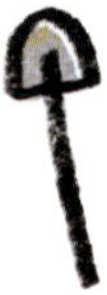

ROT'S TIPS FOR SAFE SPUDLUNKING

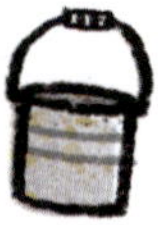

1. Call 811 first! Underground wires and pipes need to be marked before you dig in.

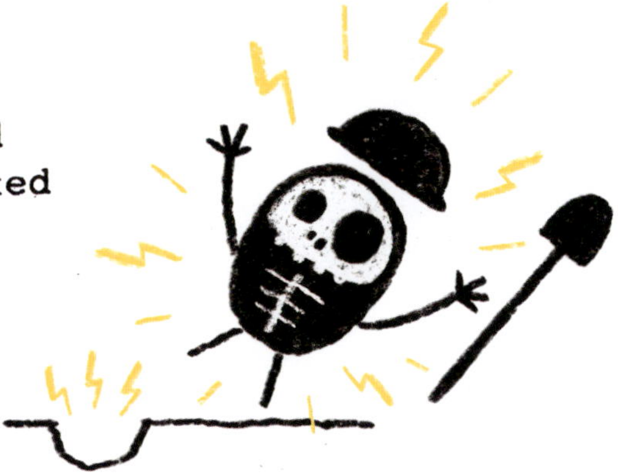

2. Respect the marks and don't dig in the dark.

3. Wear closed-toe shoes, such as boots!

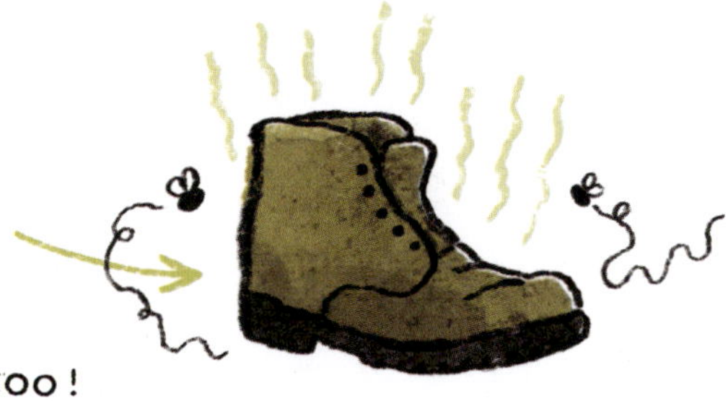

4. Gloves are good, too!

5. Make sure not to leave your shovel laying around.

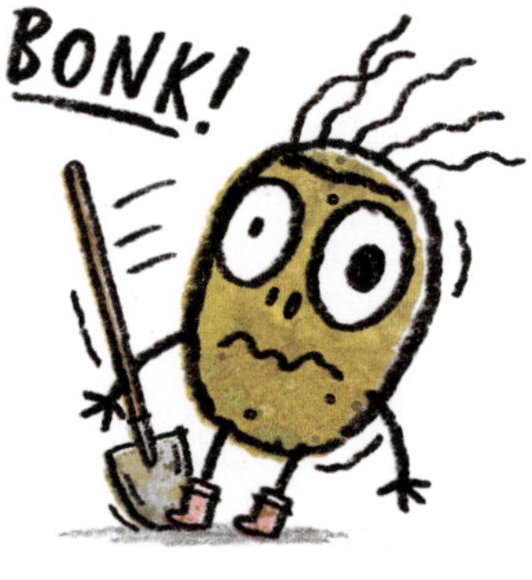
BONK!

6. Flinging dirt can be fun but not in eyes. Goggles help; plus, they look cool.

BURGUNDY'S TIPS FOR A QUALI-TEA TEA PARTY

1. Pick a fun theme. Perhaps a classic garden theme, *Alice in Wonderland*, or T. rex.

2. Send fancy invitations!

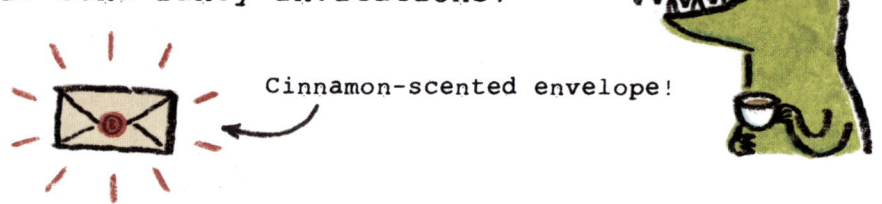

Cinnamon-scented envelope!

3. Serve a selection of teas that make you happy. I'm partial to peppermint.

4. Choose a cup and saucer perfect for each party guest.

| TOT | ROT | ROOTY | SNOT | WORM |

5. Shower your party with flowers. In vases and on plates! Little edible ones make great conversation starters.

6. Scones.

7. Scones.

ROT'S SPUDLUNKING SONG

Oh, holey moley, I'm
faster than a mole!
Yeah, I'm diggin' a hole!
Goin' ta rock 'n' roll!
Goin' ta reach my goal!
Oh! Oh! Oh! Oh! Oh! Oh! Oh! Oh!

Oh, I'm stronger
than a bull!
Yeah, I'm outta control!
Goin' ta go, go, go!
Oh! Oh! Oh! Oh! Oh! Oh! Oh! Oh!

Oh, I got diggin'
in my sole!
Yeah, it fills my bowl!
Goin' ta yo-ho-ho!
Goin' ta go low, low!
Oh! Oh! Oh! Oh! Oh! Oh! Oh! Oh!

(repeat 24 times)

TOT'S A-MAZE-ING HIDING SPOT

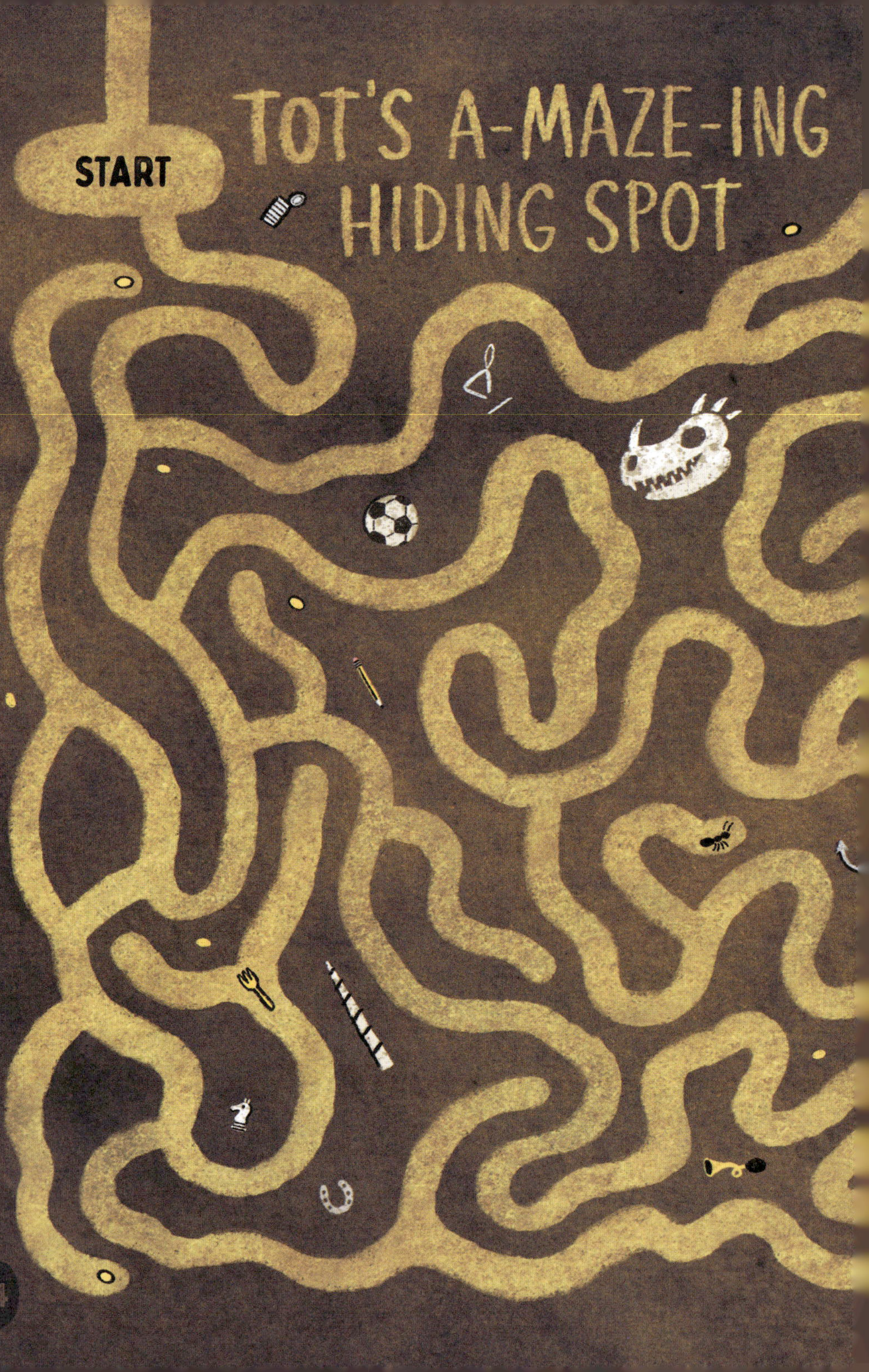
START

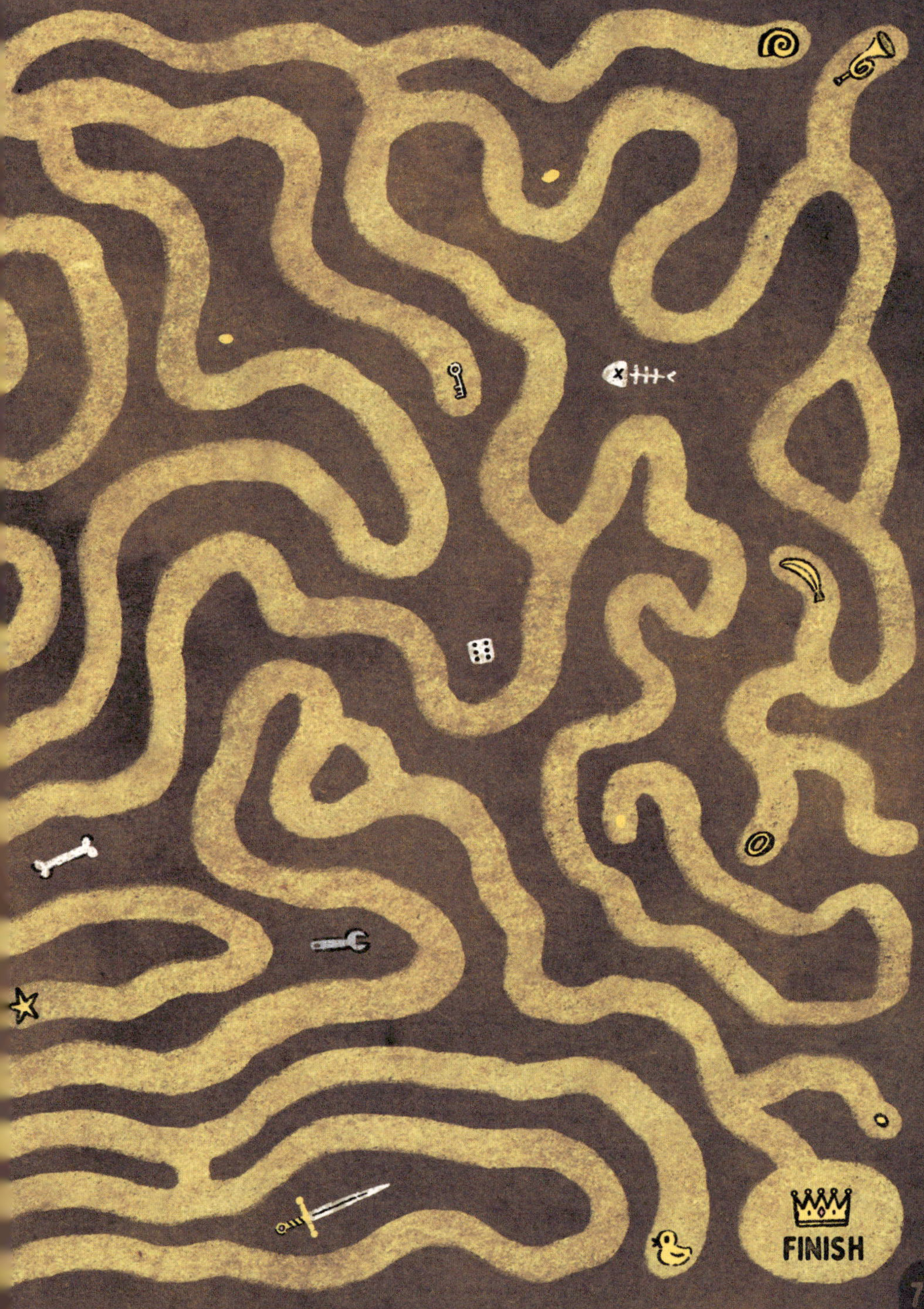
FINISH

HOW TO DRAW TOT

1
Draw a wiggly oval!

2
Eyes of great size!

3
Can you sniff out what's different?

4
Sweet smile!

5
Here you bow!

6
And add some hair up there!

7
Sticks will do the tricks for legs!

8
And arms!

9
Give yourself a hand (or two)! You did it!